WANTED,

A GENTLEMAN

KJ CHARLES

RIPTIDE
PUBLISHING

Riptide Publishing
PO Box 1537
Burnsville, NC 28714
www.riptidepublishing.com

Wanted, A Gentleman
Copyright © 2017 by KJ Charles

Cover art: Lou Harper, louharper.com/design.html
Editor: Sarah Lyons
Layout: L.C. Chase, lcchase.com/design.htm

ISBN: 978-1-62649-472-5

First edition
January, 2017

Also available in ebook:
ISBN: 978-1-62649-471-8

WANTED, A GENTLEMAN

A GENTLEMAN

KJ CHARLES

TABLE OF
CONTENTS

CHAPTER ONE

London, June 1805

W ANTED, *a GENTLEMAN. A lively and engaging Lady who finds herself in Distressing Circumstances due to her too liberal Heart seeks a Gentleman whose Kindness will be well rewarded by all the Happiness that Beauty, Congeniality, and Youth may confer. Responses to LD at the Three Ducks, Vere Street, will be most carefully consider'd.*

Beauty, congeniality, youth, and another man's child in her belly, Theo thought. Well, it happened, and the three first attributes might outweigh the last, in the event that the advertiser was telling the truth about her attractions.

Theo took leave to doubt that. In his experience, nobody told the truth until they were forced to it. But the Engaging Lady could be a foul-tempered crone for all he cared; it was none of his affair once she'd paid her shilling. He put the letter in the pile for the next issue and picked another off the day's new arrivals. There was a good haul today, a great heap of notices, all for publication in the *Matrimonial Advertiser* of Little Wild Street, proprietor Theodore Swann.

A recently widowed lady sought a man of honour and sentiment, possessed of keen wit and noble spirit, to help her regain her pleasure in life. A gentleman who had suffered reverses (through no fault of his own, he was keen to point out) would be obliged if a lady possessed of five hundred pounds would marry him before next quarter day. That was little more than a fortnight away; Theo wished him luck. An older gentleman, yet not so advanced in age that he could not enjoy life's pleasures, sought a lady of youth and buxom form. Theo was sure he did, the lecherous old goat.

The next advertisement claimed that a lady with ten thousand pounds and some beauty sought a gentleman whose elegance of mind was of more import than any concern of birth or person. She would reply to all letters. Theo rolled his eyes at that obvious fraud. Doubtless some young sprigs were having a lark at the expense of ambitious clerks dreaming of a rich wife, and more fool anyone who replied.

That was still not Theo's affair. The *Matrimonial Advertiser*'s pages had to be filled every fortnight, and if some of the advertisements were obviously false, and others self-seeking or deluded, that was none of his concern. Chaff and detritus; hopes and dreams; greed, loneliness, wishes, malice, madness, naivety: he published them all, because they paid.

He took up the next letter and his chest tightened.

A GENTLEMAN of STRONG ARM is ready & willing to chastise any handsome Youth in want of well-deserv'd Punishment. He will expect gratitude & absolute obedience in return for a stern hand with the birch.

Well, that was out of the usual run of things. Not unique—the recklessness with which some men placed advertisements astounded him—but certainly a novelty in a humdrum day. He shifted slightly in his chair, feeling a slight stir of interest. The advertisement was not for him; Theo liked his men decided and energetic, but he'd had enough chastisement of his person at school to last him a lifetime, and he had it on good authority that he was incapable of either obedience or gratitude. The Gentleman of Strong Arm would need to look elsewhere for satisfaction. Still, the words did their magic, as words always did.

The question was, could he publish it?

Perhaps. He could surely claim, if interrogated, that he'd thought the advertiser was a tutor or schoolmaster. He published everything he could, because he never turned down a shilling without regret. As long as he could reasonably claim not to have understood what was being said . . .

Theo looked at the text again. *Handsome.* Would that stand out to those who didn't know that one man might desire another, or that some found flagellation a pleasure? Would others see what was plain to his eyes? And mostly, would he find himself haled in front of the magistrates for disturbing the King's peace if he printed it?

He put the advertisement to one side of the desk for consideration and bent again to his work, pledging silently that he would go through the whole pile before he stopped for a bite to eat. He was absorbed in an eccentrically spelled paragraph from a Widdow of Refinment when a knock broke his concentration.

He looked up, but before he could speak, the door opened, without permission and with such force that the cat dozing on the windowsill levitated several inches in shock.

The man on his threshold was . . . unexpected. He was of a little more than medium height, well setup, with broad shoulders and a waist that was not trim, but certainly taut. He was also a black man.

There was nothing unfamiliar in that. Theo had lived in Marylebone during his first, despairing London years, on the cheaper outskirts of the expanding city where many black Londoners made their homes, and his nearest drinking den had been the Yorkshire Stingo, a public house greatly frequented by men of colour. He'd made friends there and had been carried along to some rousing meetings to hear speeches on the subject of slavery and abolition, often because he'd been too drunk to protest that he didn't give a fig for politics.

So it was not the visitor's colour that caught Theo's attention so much as his clothing. Most of the black men he knew were small shopkeepers and craftsmen, or jobbers like himself, making a precarious living this way and that, or beggars, or slaves. This man wore a coat that had been fitted by a good tailor not more than a few months ago, making Theo uncomfortably aware of his own dishevelled state and inky, threadbare cuffs. The visitor looked not just neat, but wealthy.

Neat, wealthy, and not at all happy. He had very thick, somewhat intimidating brows and he was fixing Theo with an unfavourable look.

Theo cleared his throat as he stood. "Good morning, sir. May I assist you?"

"I seek the publisher of the *Matrimonial Advertiser*. Mr. Swann."

The visitor had a remarkably deep voice, the kind of bass that tingled in Theo's fingers and vibrated in his chest. It would have been a very pleasurable voice to listen to if it had been a little more friendly.

"I'm Theodore Swann. At your service, sir."

"That remains to be seen," the visitor said. "My name is Martin St. Vincent, and I am here on a matter of some delicacy."

Four years of running the *Matrimonial Advertiser* had left Theo with a limited capacity for astonishment, but he was surprised now. It seemed extraordinary that this man would need to resort to advertising. There were very few women of colour in England compared to the number of men, so Mr. St. Vincent would likely enough need, or for all Theo knew might wish, to marry a white lady. Doubtless some of those would object to his complexion, but many more would not, and frankly, Theo thought, if a woman failed to appreciate the view he had now, she'd be a fool.

Martin St. Vincent was a decidedly good-looking man. He had rich, deep-brown eyes a few shades lighter than his skin, which was of a darker tint than most. Delightfully severe brows, strong cheekbones, a firm chin, and a full mouth that Theo could imagine putting to the best possible use. An impressive specimen all told, and Theo couldn't imagine why he should have to resort to advertisement, especially since his pockets were clearly well-enough filled.

Still, business was business, and if he wanted to advertise, Theo was here to take his pennies. Maybe the fellow had no graces, or intolerable breath, or the kind of character that would negate his more obvious advantages, and in that case, Theo would very happily help him conceal his faults.

"It will be my pleasure to serve," he said, slipping into his usual patter. "The *Matrimonial Advertiser* offers the greatest discretion to our patrons. We are perused by all sections of society and walks of life, and can take credit for many happy marriages—"

"You know that, do you?" enquired Mr. St. Vincent, bone-dry.

Of course Theo didn't. He had no idea how many matches he might have made, still less the happiness of the couples thus pledged. He wouldn't have wagered thruppence on it.

"Absolutely. I have many written testimonials," he assured his new client. That was perfectly true; he'd written them himself. "Our success is unparalleled. Other matrimonial gazettes cannot compare."

Mr. St. Vincent appeared profoundly unimpressed. His dark gaze travelled slowly over the shabby office and down to the heaped desk, expression quite blank, and the thought dawned on Theo rather late that perhaps he couldn't write.

That was very likely it, he decided. Illiterate men often despised the world of words that excluded them. "I will be very willing to assist you in finding the right turn of phrase, if you wish. There is an *art* of advertisement, if I can so put it, which allows a gentleman to enumerate his finer qualities and convey his hopes in the most appealing manner—"

Mr. St. Vincent looked at him. The sales patter withered on Theo's tongue.

"Are you suggesting," Mr. St. Vincent said, slowly and clearly and with just a suggestion of rigidity in his very strong jaw, "that I advertise myself? Put myself up for sale?"

Blood rushed to Theo's cheeks as the man's meaning dawned on him. "No!" he yelped, with more sincerity in that one syllable than he'd managed in this office over the last four years together. "Absolutely not, not at all, no. Not sale. Or anything else you don't want, definitely not. Uh, what *do* you want?"

Mr. St. Vincent's lips compressed, almost as if he was attempting not to smile. Theo very much hoped he would fail, mostly because he preferred it when people didn't glare at him, but in part because he rather wanted to see Mr. St. Vincent's face wearing a more pleasant expression. He essayed a hopeful smile of his own. Mr. St. Vincent's eyelids drooped disdainfully.

"What I want, Mr. Swann, is information." He stepped forward, holding a copy of the last issue of the *Advertiser* out, over the desk. A message was circled in ink.

CRESSIDA—Your words gladden my soul. My most ardent sentiments grow stronger daily. They cannot separate us forever. Let me know your heart when you can—Your TROILUS

Troilus and Cressida's correspondence had appeared in the *Matrimonial Advertiser* for a number of issues now, with declarations of love, plaints against cruel fate and restrictive guardians, and cryptic instructions for further communication. Theo's impression of Cressida was of a young lady thoroughly enjoying herself. He read the advertisement over again. "Yes?"

"Well?"

"Uh . . ." Well, what? Theo scrabbled to find the answer he was clearly expected to give, and came up with, "Are you Troilus?"

Mr. St. Vincent looked at him. "No."

"Cressida?" Theo's mouth suggested, before his brain could step in to prevent it.

"Let's come to an arrangement," Mr. St. Vincent said. "You tell me everything you know about this Troilus, and I won't bring two men with cudgels to make you."

"Oh. Are you Cressida's father?" He seemed a little young for the role, around thirty by Theo's guess, but boys made mistakes. Theo certainly had, although not that one.

"No. Stop asking me questions, Mr. Swann. Your role is to give answers."

Theo retrieved his professional smile from somewhere, not without effort. He was quite used to being spoken to with distaste, but it didn't usually happen here, where he worked and slept. Swallowing insult in his own home rankled.

"Sir, you will understand that confidentiality is crucial to my business. There is no dishonour in this means of seeking a companion, but it can be met by a sad lack of sympathy." Mr. St. Vincent's snort suggested he was among the unsympathetic. "And I cannot disclose private affairs," Theo finished in a rush. "Well, but consider, sir, I have promised discretion—"

"And you are a man who always keeps his promises, I have no doubt. Let us not play games. How much for your loyalty?"

Mr. St. Vincent's tone was so sardonic that it brought the blood flaming to Theo's face. How dare he? How dare the fellow walk in here and weigh him up and in just a couple of moments decide that Theo was untrustworthy, unreliable, ready to be bought?

He was, of course. But how dare this man just *assume* it, with that lazily dismissive look in his eyes?

He'd double the price for that, Theo thought vengefully, and had to remind himself of the men with cudgels. He didn't doubt their existence—he'd been threatened similarly more than once—and he had no desire to encounter them.

And pride was not something Theo could afford. If his visitor was truly offering a carrot as well as a stick, he would do well to take the former.

"Look here, Mr. St. Vincent," he said, dropping the high-flown talk since it wasn't working, and going for the air of an honest, plainspoken man. "I take the advertisements, I lay them out, I publish the *Advertiser*. All that's lawful enough. If there's something unlawful being conducted in my pages, I'd like to know what. I won't have that sort of thing."

"Will you not." Mr. St. Vincent picked up a paper from the desk. It was, Theo realised, the advertisement from the Gentleman of Strong Arm, and he'd apparently read it upside down.

Well, bollocks.

"I shan't publish that one, of course," he said. "Dear me. What people send, Mr. St. Vincent, you'd be amazed."

"Mmm." Mr. St. Vincent's eyes were fixed on the paper. This close, Theo could see they weren't a plain brown, but flecked with glinting orange, like one of those semiprecious stones. Topaz, he thought it might be called, or possibly agate. He decided on topaz, as the lovelier word.

Not that Mr. St. Vincent seemed lovely as he read aloud, in frozen tones, "'Ready & willing to chastise any handsome Youth in want of well-deserv'd Punishment.' Well, there's plenty of people in want of that. Out of interest, Mr. Swann, if I read through your back issues, how many advertisements of this sort would I find?"

Enough to bring me all the trouble you wish, was the answer. Theo braced himself for the threat that would follow.

It didn't come. Mr. St. Vincent dropped the paper to the desk. "What a trade you have, sir. Very well." He indicated the advertisement he'd circled. "The lady here called Cressida is just turned seventeen years old and possessed of a strong will and determined temper. She has been engaging in a clandestine correspondence with this 'Troilus' for months. Troilus claims to be a gentleman and honourable in his intentions, but he has made no approach to the lady's father, who discovered this business only by accident. He is an extremely wealthy man, and she his only child."

"Ah."

"Indeed. Miss— Cressida is to be presented at Court next season," Mr. St. Vincent went on. "She is likely to make an excellent match, with her own charms and her father's wealth. You may imagine that he does not want her snatched away by a fortune hunter before she is out."

Theo could, although it was nothing more than imagination. He had not mixed in circles of wealth or rank even before he had been cast out to the darkness of London; he had nothing to do with Society here in his shabby, precarious refuge on Little Wild Street. "I daresay he does not. But with respect, is that not a matter for him alone? Should he not assert his, uh, paternal authority over the lady?"

"She is of *very* strong will, and *extremely* determined temper," Mr. St. Vincent said drily. "The correspondence was discovered, so the young lady was removed from her school. Her letters were inspected, so she bribed a maid to deliver them in secret. The maid was dismissed, but then—" he tapped the circled advertisement "—this. Since it appears her family can't stop her, I have been charged with the task of stopping him."

That wasn't entirely clear. "You're the family's servant?" The man seemed too well dressed for a household position, but why else would he be entrusted with such a sensitive task?

"I'm a merchant," Mr. St. Vincent said, voice even. "My help was asked as a trusted friend of the family. As a favour."

Theo filed that away for future reference. Mr. St. Vincent's relationship to the family was of no great interest to him; what mattered was that if the fellow had been asked to deal with a matter of such delicacy, he would surely want to succeed. He would be very ready to do whatever was needed, which would doubtless include paying for assistance. And if there was money in it, Theo was interested.

"Well, that puts matters in a different light," he said. "Obviously, in law, the lady is entitled to place whatever advertisement she wishes, but her father's concern is most natural, and I should not wish any match made in the pages of the *Matrimonial Advertiser* to be less than happy. I can, I think, aid you a little more than somewhat. The only question is— I hesitate to ask it in a matter of such importance, but you will understand that my work is demanding and my time precious. Of course it is my earnest wish to help, but as a mere publisher, supporting myself wholly by my labour—"

"How much?"

"Two guineas."

"Five shillings."

"One guinea."

"Ten shillings, and don't argue with me," said Mr. St. Vincent with finality.

Less than Theo had hoped, better than he'd feared. "Done."

"Right. Who is he?"

"I've no idea." Theo held up his hands against the other man's look. "I'm not given names. People want discretion."

"What about letters? How are they exchanged?"

"They come to the public house I use—"

"The Three Ducks."

Theo shifted in his seat at the implication he thought he heard. "It's the closest by. And Ducks, you see, so people remember it. Because of Swann. My name." Mr. St. Vincent's expression suggested he had not needed that explained in quite so much detail. Theo pulled himself together. "I don't see the letters coming in or handed out; the publican does all that. Was the lady writing to Troilus as well as advertising?"

"It appears there was some direct correspondence recently, thanks to the bootboy. Miss Cressida has loyal friends, and a talent for suborning the staff." There was just a slight curve to his lips as he said that, a glimmer of reluctant amusement. "A letter from Troilus was found among her possessions, but bore no address."

Theo applauded Troilus's caution; he wouldn't risk putting his own address on clandestine correspondence either, for fear of finding those men with cudgels at his door. "Well, if Miss Cressida sent letters via the Ducks, it's possible the landlord may recall who came asking for them. I can take you there to find out."

"And?"

"And what?"

Mr. St. Vincent gave him a look. "Are you proposing to charge me ten shillings merely to take me to an inn?"

"I can do more," Theo offered hastily. "Just let me see." He glanced around, identified the pile of waste paper he had yet to discard, and went to scrabble through it. "A moment, a moment—here!" He held up the object of his search. "Troilus's most recent advertisement. This will appear in tomorrow's *Advertiser*."

"'CRESSIDA,'" Mr. St. Vincent read aloud. "'My sentiments of admiration and respect can be confined no longer. You have my heart. May I dream to have your hand? Reply to your TROILUS in *The Times*.' The wretch." His hand closed on the paper. "You will not publish this."

"I can't stop it," Theo said. "The papers have been printed and collected."

"Recall them."

"I can't!" The thought alone was enough to make him sweat at the expense it would entail. "It's impossible. And anyway, surely you don't want me to?"

"I believe I expressed myself clearly," Mr. St. Vincent said.

"No, but hear me out. It seems as though your lovebirds have done very well at finding ways to communicate. If you cut off this route, will they not find another you don't expect? If I were him, I'd put this in half a dozen papers, actually. Make sure she sees it. In any case, if this advertisement appears, you will know Miss Cressida's next move. Even if you fail to intercept her response, you can watch the columns of *The Times*."

"I see," Mr. St. Vincent said slowly. "Yes. Very well."

"And it's his writing," Theo added. "That is the hand in which all his advertisements have been written." The adequately formed script of an adequately educated man, lacking any individuality, as though the writer had not cared to write much since he left the schoolroom. "If it comes to a matter at law, or of identification . . ."

"I see. Good. You're earning your fee, Mr. Swann," Mr. St. Vincent said, with a hint of surprise. Theo had a vague urge to kick him. "Now you can earn it a little more."

"Absolutely. I shall be delighted. How?"

"By taking me to an inn, of course."

Martin paced down Little Wild Street with Swann at his side, keeping one eye on his companion. He believed the man's story, for what that was worth, but he had no intention of paying the ten shillings before they were fairly earned. He did not trust Theodore

Swann as far as he could throw him, although that would probably be a reasonable distance, the puny wretch that he was.

A down-at-heel sort of man, Theodore Swann. Worn, ink-stained cuffs and a coat whose better days had long passed and not been particularly good in the first place. Perhaps four inches shorter than himself, and built on much less sturdy lines, with a thin, pale, bony face, narrow shoulders, and flyaway light-brown hair. His voice was decidedly more educated than his appearance suggested; his grey eyes, the colour of wet weather, were calculating; his manner was wheedling. He was quite clearly a grasping, untrustworthy, venal man who carried out a trade that Martin regarded with baffled disdain.

He looked as though he'd fuck like a tomcat.

It was an absurd thought, a dangerous thought, and what was worse, it wasn't impossible. There was that intangible *something* about Swann that had Martin's own awareness tingling, but more, too—that advertisement sitting on his desk, and the fact Swann had very clearly known what it meant. And of course he used the Three Ducks inn.

Granted, it was no distance from the shabby, cluttered office on Little Wild Street to Vere Street, where the Three Ducks stood. It was quite natural that the *Matrimonial Advertiser*'s letters should be delivered to the public house there. But Martin knew exactly what sort of place the Three Ducks was, and he had little doubt that Swann did too.

Little doubt of that; no doubt at all that Swann would use anything he might find about Martin for his own ends, which made it all the more imperative he keep his thoughts to himself.

He could do that. Very few people ever suspected his tastes ran to men, so far as he could tell, and it would surely not be hard to keep his hands off a fellow whose face suggested he'd sell his own grandmother. Even if there was that *something* about him that set Martin's imagination off and running.

Because of course Swann did sell people, or at least offer a market for them to sell themselves. Men advertising for rich women, women advertising for men to keep them or buy them. The business turned Martin's stomach, and it was Swann's living.

And now it was Martin's problem, because of Miss Jennifer Conroy.

He found it difficult to think about the Conroys clearly. He had no idea how to unpick the decades-old knot of anger, resentment, obligation, love, and hate that tied him to the family. But Miss Jennifer was just seventeen and the object of an obviously unscrupulous man's attentions, and Martin had no doubt what he felt about that.

He'd been thirteen when Miss Jennifer was born. He'd carried her, sung to her, read her stories, played pat-a-cake with her chubby hands, and rioted around her nursery being a horse, bear, dragon, or anything else required by her imperious demands as she grew, because the unquestioning, uncomplicated love of a child had been an anchor to something good and right in his life, even as he'd grown to manhood and his anger had grown with him.

It had ended when he was eighteen. He'd left the Conroys then, and it would hardly have been appropriate for a grown man of no family or fortune to play with a child-heiress, even had he not been busy making a life for himself. He'd become a free man with responsibilities. But he had never forgotten those games, that little golden time of simple childhood, and the thought of Miss Jennifer hurling herself into the arms of some greasy, greedy fraud was appalling. A married woman was subject to her husband's whim or command. Her property became his to use or waste, her body his to command and chastise; her husband was legally her master. Martin wondered why any free woman would subject herself to it, given a choice.

Miss Jennifer would doubtless marry, because that was what young ladies did, but at least she would not have to tie herself to some brute from necessity. Her wealth was a honeypot that would attract an extensive range of potential husbands from which she might have her pick. Unfortunately, like all honeypots, it attracted wasps too.

They had reached the Three Ducks while he wool-gathered. Swann glanced up at him. "I could fetch Mr. Royle out here, if you prefer?"

Martin considered that. It might be wise not to enter a known sodomites' den at all, and certainly not with Theodore Swann. His eyes were a little too searching for that, his manner a little too much on the lookout for advantage, and Martin just a little too aware of his lean body. On the other hand, his throat was dry, it was uncomfortably hot, and they were about the Conroys' private business, which was not to be conducted in the street.

"We'll go in."

The interior of the Three Ducks was dark and cool. There were only a few men in there, all white, of course, and doubtless most of them hoping to find willing flesh. Everyone looked around as the door opened. A couple saluted Swann; a few more gave Martin long, speculative examinations. He sensed curiosity rather than hostility, but found that hardly more welcome. He was very, very tired of being the object of curiosity.

Martin took a seat at one end of a heavy wooden bench sticky with years of spilled beer, as Swann went to the bar and returned with a couple of pints of ale. "Mr. Royle will be with us shortly. He may be able to tell you something of who came for the letters. A name like Troilus might be sufficiently unusual to have snagged his attention."

Martin sipped the thin ale and grimaced. Swann gave an apologetic shrug.

"Why do you do it?" Martin asked at last, just to break the silence.

"What?"

"Your paper. Why advertise marriage?"

"Why not? It pays. People want to find husbands and wives, so why should they not seek them?"

"It's . . ." Martin searched for the word. "Lowering. Commercial."

"Well, we are all commercial. This is the age of commerce. A man is worth his value at the bank."

"I know what a man is worth," Martin said, the words tasting as sour as the beer.

Swann's eyes snapped up to meet his gaze. "Well, yes, but . . . That is, are you married or affianced?"

"No."

"Would you like to be?"

Martin gave him a look. "If you intend to play Cupid with me—"

"I shouldn't dream of it. Unless you pay me to, in which case I shall be delighted. But the fact is, most people *would* like to be married, and this is the modern world. We must all make our own way. I simply provide a service by which people may encounter one another and form their own arrangements."

"As this Troilus is trying to do."

Swann turned his palms up. "He wants a rich wife. Do you blame him for that? You may fault his way of going about it, but you can hardly argue with his ambition. You said yourself that Miss Cressida's riches ought to secure her a good husband—which, put the other way, is to say that a well-born man will choose her because of her riches. Well, then, where is the difference? She is to be married for her money either way. The only difference is whether she chooses for herself or her father does it for her. And as I say, this is the modern world. May not a lady have a voice in her own future?"

Martin sought for a riposte. He couldn't immediately find one, a fact that did not make him feel any more kindly disposed to Swann. "Her parents want a husband who will treat her well. Who will offer affection, and value her for more than her money."

"Oh, I see. So they don't intend to marry her to the highest-ranking man they can snare?"

"It's none of your damned affair what they intend," Martin snapped, since he well knew that a title was the peak of Mrs. Conroy's ambition.

Swann shrugged. "All I say is, marriage is a business same as any other, and everyone's got the right to pursue his own advancement. Or hers."

"And yours with it, since you make a profit from their efforts."

"You don't make a profit from your business?" Swann asked with wide-eyed concern. "Perhaps you should have someone help you with that."

Martin was saved from responding by the approach of a greasy fellow in a greasy apron. He introduced himself as Royle, the landlord, who collected and distributed letters on Swann's behalf.

"Troilus, Troilus," he muttered. "Aye, I recall the fellow, he came a few times in a fortnight or so. Tall, thin drink of water. Right miserable, too, not a pleasant word spoke."

"Do you have a name?" Martin asked. The landlord shrugged. "Can you describe him?"

"Tall. Thin."

Martin sighed. "Face?"

"Aye, he had one," Royle said, and broke into a wheezy laugh. Swann cackled. Martin glowered at them both. "I dunno. Nose in the air sort of cove."

"Hair?"

"How should I know?"

"Because you saw him," Martin said. "Don't play the fool with me."

"Aye, I saw him, but I didn't see under his wig, did I?"

"Wig?"

"Aye, wig. Horsehair. The usual thing."

"He was a servant?" Swann demanded.

"Didn't I say?"

"No," Martin said, with restraint. "You didn't."

"Oh, well. Footman, I reckon, or some such."

He could describe nothing else, didn't know where the footman had come from or gone to, had nothing else to offer that might help, and wandered off after a little more fruitless conversation to give the bar a desultory wipe with a dirty cloth.

Martin and Swann looked at each other. "Servant."

"Acting on his own behalf?" Swann mused. "Or doing his master's bidding?"

"If Troilus is a gentleman . . ." Martin began slowly.

"That'd be bad, wouldn't it? For the family, I mean."

"How do you work that out?"

"Well, one—" Swann counted on a finger "—he likely isn't the sort of gentleman you'd want for a son-in-law, or he'd have put his suit to Old Mr. Cressida, not managed things this havey-cavey way with secret letters. He must know he'd be given his marching orders if he went about matters directly. But, two, if he appears and sounds a gentleman, he's more likely to win the lady's agreement. Wouldn't you say?"

Martin had been assuming Troilus was some hopeful clerk, likely to be a threat to Miss Conroy's reputation because of their clandestine correspondence rather than a serious danger to her heart. The picture Swann had painted was significantly more worrying. "Yes. I see."

"And the other thing is . . ." Swann counted off a third finger. "If he can pay a servant, he can probably pay for other things. Like a special licence, say—no, she's too young for that. But certainly money will make things easier for him. It always does."

Martin gave him a long look. "You seem to have thought about this a great deal, considering you claim not to know anything about Troilus."

"I've never thought about him in my life," Swann said indignantly. "I can tell a hawk from a handsaw, that's all. You tell me there's a rich lady and a fellow wooing her for her money, and then you wonder why I can imagine what happens next?"

"All right, that's fair." Martin subsided a little.

"I'm a scribbler, when I'm not running the *Advertiser*," Swann added. "Making stories is my trade." He hesitated. "And I know plenty of others in the same trade. Gossipmongers. If your young lady is wealthy as you say, word might have spread of this. If I knew the lady's name, I could ask—"

"No."

Swann held his hands up in surrender. "Your choice. Very well, then, I suppose you've to wait for her reply in *The Times* and see where you go from there. So, Mr. St. Vincent." He tipped up his pint mug, drank, licked ale from his lips with a pink, pointed tongue. "What else will you have from me for your money?"

The question caught Martin completely unaware. He'd been focused on the problem at hand, and on Swann's words and the agile mind they revealed. He hadn't been thinking of Swann's thin, sinewy body at all for the last few minutes, but he bloody was now.

He knew exactly what he'd like from this ratty, unscrupulous little sod, in this dark den with its darker back room and a landlord whose business and freedom depended on discretion. His hands on Swann's sharp hip bones, or tangled in his hair, or pressing down on that lean back that would look so pale in the shadows, and feeling Swann push against his strength.

It was what he'd like, and he was sure it was what he could have for, at most, an extra few shillings. Swann, bought and paid for.

He shoved the bench away from the table with a grinding scrape. "Just find a way to earn it."

CHAPTER TWO

Theo glared down at the blank page. It looked back at him with studied disinterest.

It was four days since Martin St. Vincent had brought his distracting presence into the office. In the interim, Theo had done his best to earn the promised ten shillings. He'd kept a weather eye out for any letters, to his office or the Three Ducks; examined the other newspapers and rival matrimonial gazettes in case the errant couple were advertising in more than one forum; even gone through back issues of the *Matrimonial Advertiser* looking for clues and finding none. He hadn't seen hide or hair of St. Vincent in all that time.

He *had* identified Cressida, though, not that such had been part of his commission. She was Miss Jennifer Conroy, daughter of an immensely wealthy plantation owner whose new house on Cavendish Square had been designed by the great Nash. Her identity was probably not something St. Vincent would want him to know.

It hadn't been difficult to discover. St. Vincent had been discreet in everything except his own name, but a black man surnamed for a Caribbean island? Theo had started by looking at the wealthiest plantation owners whose money came from the West Indies, found four with a single daughter, and then simply asked a few people in their households: *Did you once have a Martin St. Vincent here?*

He'd been a slave. Theo wasn't surprised by that, but he was disturbed on a deep, rather sick level to think of it, and he wasn't quite sure why. He knew plenty of men who were or had been enslaved. That was how things were, and while Theo didn't buy slave sugar on the few occasions he could afford sugar at all, and would have spoken for abolition if anyone had asked his opinion, he was not one to fight against the world. It wasn't, in the end, his problem. He could shrug and move on. He always did.

He had a feeling that St. Vincent was not the sort of man who shrugged. There was a simmering deep-down anger there that Theo recognised, the kind that made you not want to cross a man in case it erupted. The kind that said, *I do not forgive lightly.*

That being the case, why was he working for his former masters? Theo had drifted up to his old drinking haunt in Marylebone, the Yorkshire Stingo, which functioned not only as a public house but also as a sort of poor relief for men and women of colour in distress. That was where you'd go to ask about a black Londoner, and he'd found out enough about Martin St. Vincent to chew on. It seemed he was doing well enough for himself. He was a dealer in coal, invested in a number of small businesses and coffeehouses owned by men and women of his own race, and from what Theo could gather, he was a successful and respected, if rather solitary, man. He attended abolitionist meetings, though he never spoke, and contributed generously to the Stingo's much-needed relief fund for the hungry, the homeless, the men abandoned to the streets after they'd been beaten or worked half to death.

Meanwhile, the Conroys lived in luxury on the proceeds of plantations tilled by slave labour, yet St. Vincent called himself the family's friend. Theo couldn't understand that.

Couldn't, and was wasting his time trying to. The fact was, Martin St. Vincent was none of Theo's affair. His task was not to puzzle over St. Vincent's motivations, no matter how curious he might be, or how memorable he found those orange-flecked eyes. His job was to extricate Miss Adelina Fanshawe from the clutches of her dastardly guardian's last desperate effort to force a marriage, and reunite her with the strong, clean-limbed, ineffably dull Thomas Mountjoy before the end of the week, when their romance was due at his publisher.

Theo sincerely hoped his readers would find Mountjoy less boring than he did. He could barely stand the fellow himself, and Adelina was almost as bad. They deserved each other, the ghastly, virtuous, pallid pair. He was tempted to kill them off—a sudden earthquake would be satisfying—and leave Adelina's guardian

Jasper de Vere triumphant, with his faithful hunchbacked henchman by his side. Theo had some fairly clear ideas about Jasper and his henchman, and indeed he had mentally played them out alone in bed with his hand's assistance, but it was scarcely a story he could write for money, and that was why he wrote, as it was why he did everything.

Adelina: or, Virtue Imperill'd would soon go out to add to the body of work that he offered a mildly interested world under the barely disguised persona of Dorothea Swann. Mrs. Swann was making a modest name for herself as an authoress of Gothic romances, in the spirit of Mrs. Radcliffe although without her sales quite yet. If Theo could just get Adelina and her damned virtue off his desk early, he could make a start on his new story before the next issue of the *Advertiser* had to be prepared. All he had to do was invent something clever for Thomas Mountjoy to do—*hah*—and stop thinking about Martin St. Vincent, and his eyes, and what he might look like if he really smiled.

Although Theo could have sworn, in the Three Ducks, just for a moment . . .

"Oh, stop it," he said aloud, and dipped his pen with such determination that tiny droplets of ink flew.

He'd managed a full paragraph of veiled threats to Adelina's well-being before the newsboy's cry echoed up from Little Wild Street. Theo couldn't miss it, since his window was open even at this hour because of the summer heat. *The Times* was out.

Cressida—Miss Jennifer Conroy, rather—had not managed to reply to the last advertisement in any way that he had seen in the last few days. Perhaps she was being more closely watched, or had had some sense knocked into her. Still, Theo was, he hoped, being paid, and for that he could be vigilant. He leaned out of the window, careful not to disturb the ever-present, ever-sleeping cat, shouted for a copy of the paper, and ran down to collect it.

As always *The Times* was full of advertisements in close-printed type: personal, legal, commercial, matrimonial. He skimmed his way through and came to a dead stop.

CRESSIDA—Why have I to endure her obstinate refusal? Sentiment eternal can earn love. Let affection rule today—TROILUS

"What the tits?" he said aloud.

He couldn't make out what Troilus was bleating about. Had he been rejected? Was he talking about some response from Cressida that Theo had missed? And was she really retreating from the field? She had hardly seemed obstinate before in her advertisements, but maybe the girl had more sense than St. Vincent or her father credited.

That must be it. Troilus had been turned down and was making a last stab at a rich bride with this promise of eternal love. Theo could have written a better plea with his left hand and blindfold, but the point was, this was not the message of a successful suitor. Theo would not be required further, he would be lucky to get the promised ten shillings for the little he'd achieved, and he wouldn't see Martin St. Vincent again.

The man hadn't even liked him. That much had been obvious. St. Vincent evidently had a strong moral streak—he was a regular churchgoer according to the gossips in the Stingo—and though Theo would swear he'd been tempted in the Three Ducks (that look of shock when Theo had offered to earn his wage, the way his orange-flecked eyes had widened . . .) he'd had no trouble resisting. He'd given Theo his card, with an address, but the greatest optimist could not have interpreted the way he'd done it as an invitation.

No: it had been a strange but fruitless interlude, and all Theo was likely to get from it was, if he was lucky, some fodder for a future plot.

Perhaps even the solution to Adelina's problem, now he thought of it. Perhaps she might bribe a servant to place an advertisement in the newspaper and alert Thomas What-the-devil-was-his-name to her plight that way? Rather than sending him a letter directly, of course, because . . . he scrabbled for a reason . . . because *something*, he'd work it out later. Maybe the servant insisted on reading her letters, that might be it, and it had to be disguised as an innocuous advertisement. Which Adelina would need to be ingenious enough to write, and Thomas to decipher, so it would have to be a damned simple code for that pair of imbeciles.

He bent back to his task, doggedly pushing out the whirling, fast-paced adventure word by tedious word.

Theo wrote until the clocks were chiming five in the afternoon. His hand was sore and his cuffs blackened, but Adelina's deliverance was well underway at last, and he had come up with a peculiarly ingenious demise for Jasper that almost resigned him to killing the fellow.

He stood, stretched, feeling the day's writing in the stiffness of his back and shoulders, and took the newspaper to the chophouse around the corner, where he dined substantially, if not particularly well, on steak-and-kidney pudding, and then indulged himself with a second glass of ale. It was that or the more dangerous indulgence of going to the Three Ducks, or somewhere like it, and scratching the itch that he'd had ever since Martin St. Blasted Vincent walked in to disturb his work.

He'd left *The Times* folded to the page of Troilus's advertisement, and now read it again, with justifiable annoyance. If the fellow had only said something sensible, such as, *Run away with me tonight, my love*, he would have had an excuse to seek St. Vincent out. In order to do something useful and earn the ten shillings, obviously.

CRESSIDA—Why have I to endure her obstinate refusal? Sentiment eternal can earn love. Let affection rule today—TROILUS

Theo felt a prickle of irritation, made worse by a twinge of sympathy. If he had learned anything in the last seven years, it was that pleading or whining at scorn was the most pointless, self-defeating thing a man could do. *Grit your teeth and accept it*, he wanted to tell Troilus. *If you beg, they will only despise you more, and hate you too for the embarrassment you cause them. Believe me. I've tried.*

And if a man *had* to grovel, he should do it better than this incoherent rubbish. Particularly that irritating cod-poetic switch of persons, speaking of the woman and then directly addressing her in the next line. What was that meant to achieve? Why had Troilus needed *her* instead of *your* there?

Theo looked at the advertisement. He looked again. He sat with the pint mug halfway to his lips, unable to move for a few seconds because the inspiration was too blinding white behind his eyes to allow for anything else. Then he threw a few pennies onto the table, scooped up the paper, and ran.

St. Vincent's card gave an address in Marylebone, on the outer edge of the city sprawl, not far from where Theo had used to live. He wondered if they'd crossed each other's paths, unnoticing, though he did think he might have remembered St. Vincent.

It was perhaps a mile and a half from his current home on Little Wild Street. Theo ran much of the way in the still-hot late-afternoon air, and was gasping and more dishevelled than usual when he finally seized St. Vincent's door knocker, hanging on to it as much as rapping.

The door was opened by a woman dressed as a housekeeper. A rather attractive woman in her early twenties, come to that, somewhat lighter-skinned than St. Vincent, with a pair of lively eyes that examined Theo searchingly as he urgently requested the master of the house, and reached a less-than-favourable conclusion. He couldn't blame her, sweaty as he was.

She showed him into the parlour with a forbidding look that suggested she'd count the spoons after his departure, and a few moments later St. Vincent himself arrived. He was wearing loose breeches and a thin white linen shirt shaded by the darker skin it covered. His shirtsleeves were rolled up against the heat, baring forearms that Theo wanted, suddenly and urgently, to squeeze between his thighs, and the open neck of the shirt revealed the hollow at the base of his throat. There was a little dark mark there, a black pinprick, a beauty spot that drew Theo's eyes as he tried to gather himself.

"Mr. Swann?" St. Vincent sounded not quite unfriendly, but certainly wary and a little startled. "What on earth—"

"*The Times.*" Theo brandished the paper. "Advertisement."

"I saw it. It is nonsense."

"It's not. It's a message."

"What message?" St. Vincent's voice was sharp and concerned. He was listening, not arguing or dismissing, and it gave Theo an absurd jolt of satisfaction.

"The initial letters. The words don't matter, it's the initials."

St. Vincent seized the newspaper. "W-h-i-t-e . . . white horse cellar-t?" he asked aloud, and then corrected himself. "No. 'White Horse Cellar. Today. Troilus.' Hell's teeth. A rendezvous?"

Theo nodded frantically. "The White Horse Cellar in Piccadilly. It's a coaching inn, the stages go from there."

"So they could pass unnoticed in the bustle? Oh, devil take it."

"Well, that, but . . ." Theo took a breath, as much from nerves as need. "With the greatest respect to the lady, it's quarter day in a fortnight."

"What has that to do with anything?"

"That it's the day for settling debts."

St. Vincent, the merchant, gave him a look. "Yes, I am aware of that. The lady has no debts."

"I meant Troilus," Theo said. "He didn't approach the lady's parents in the proper manner, yet a footman collected his letters. Suppose he's a gentleman with pockets to let, urgent obligations to meet before settling day. Suppose he needs a rich wife quickly."

St. Vincent's eyes widened. "You think he intends Gretna Green?"

"There can be no marriage in England without her father's consent. I daresay an unscrupulous man might compromise her, to force her parents to agree to a wedding. But a dash to Gretna and a legal marriage, to give him a wealthy father-in-law, like it or not—"

St. Vincent grabbed his wrist. His fingers were warm and tight on Theo's skin. "Come on."

"Where to? The Cellar, or her home? Has she even gone, do you know?"

"No, I don't." St. Vincent hesitated. "Curse it. There's no time to lose if she has. Very well. I'll go to the house, find if she's still there. And in case she's not—"

"I'll go to the White Horse Cellar now," Theo completed. Aside from wanting to earn his money, he wouldn't miss an opportunity to see a genuine elopement for the world. "What description? I daresay she won't use her name."

"I sincerely hope not. She's seventeen, not tall for a woman. Perhaps about your height."

"Thank you *so* much."

"Brown hair with a deal of curl to it, blue eyes, and a very . . ." He seemed to search for a word. "A notably up-tilted nose."

"Right. If I find anything out, if it seems she did go there, where shall I meet you?" St. Vincent hesitated, evidently uncertain as to his answer. Theo sighed. "Should I come to the Conroys' house on Cavendish Square?"

"*What?*"

"It really wasn't hard to find out," Theo said. "I was trying to make myself useful."

"Unless it is absolutely urgent, meet me back here," St. Vincent said. "If the Conroys discover you're the publisher of that accursed gazette, they'll probably have you horsewhipped."

Theo sniffed. "Charming."

St. Vincent's warm grip tightened on his wrist. "*I* am grateful for this." His voice really was deliciously deep. "That you saw it, understood it, and brought it to me. Thank you."

"I should hope so," Theo mumbled, for lack of a better response.

"Now get on." St. Vincent released him with a little push. "We may not have much time."

Any hope that Martin had cherished of Swann being wrong, or Miss Jennifer either being thwarted in her romantic plans or simply exhibiting whatever sense she'd been born with, were dashed as he stepped out of the hackney onto Cavendish Square. Conroy House was frantic with action. Servants hurried in and out in a display of pointless activity that Martin suspected sprang from Mr. Conroy's habitual cry of, "Well, *do* something!"

He exchanged a nod with the footman at the open door. His relationship with the Conroys' staff was an uneasy one. He had been at once above and below the servants during his childhood, treated with the fond indulgence one might give a household pet, yet still and always less than the humblest of the kitchen maids. The maids had been free to leave. Free to starve if they left, true, while Martin had been well-fed and clothed at the master's expense. He'd had an education none of them could have hoped for. But still, they had been free.

Martin was now an independent man and counted by the family as a friend, if not an equal one. He had his own business, his own home. But he had once had less than nothing and that was not forgotten.

"I must see Mr. Conroy at once," he said. "It's regarding Miss Jennifer."

"You're a bit late for that," the footman said under his breath.

"She's not here?" The man tipped his head. Martin clenched his fist, cursing that he had not accompanied Swann to the public house in Piccadilly. "Tell them I've called. *Now*, man. I know where she's gone."

He waited in the perfectly proportioned, lavishly decorated hall, still gleaming new. It had been a relief when the Conroys had moved here, away from the house in which he had grown up. He could walk in here without feeling the old, tight weight closing around his neck.

He was admitted to the opulent drawing room within minutes. Mrs. Conroy rocked on the couch, face blotchy with tears and distorted with grief. Mr. Conroy was pacing, his whole body tense. They both looked round as he came in.

"Mr. Conroy, Mrs. Conroy. Has Miss Jennifer gone?"

"Martin." Mr. Conroy strode towards him. "Have you heard something? What do you know?"

Martin. Always the Christian name. Even the unadorned *St. Vincent* would be better than his Christian name, used as one would speak to a child or a servant.

And it was hardly the time to stew over an unintended slight, while their daughter was heaven knew where with heaven knew who. "Is it true? Do you know where she is?"

"No. We don't." Mrs. Conroy's fingers knotted together in a way that looked painful. "She hasn't been seen since two o'clock. She retired to her room with the headache. And she isn't there. Nobody knows where she went, nobody has had word—"

Martin checked that he had shut the door. "I am sorry to say this, but I think she may have gone to meet her correspondent. Troilus."

"How dare you!" said Mr. Conroy, explosively and angrily, as Mrs. Conroy said, "No. She has not. You cannot say so. She has *not*."

Martin was not surprised at their reaction. Lively, pretty, indulged Miss Jennifer was the joy of her parents' souls. Mrs. Conroy had dreamed of her daughter's first Season and grand marriage for years. Mr. Conroy kept at his business, even though his heart was troublesome and his dyspepsia an agony, so that Miss Jennifer's dowry would be second to none. Everything they did was for Miss Jennifer's good. Every slave condemned to the sugarcane fields, every back marked by whips, was a sacrifice to Miss Jennifer for the glittering future it now seemed she was throwing away.

"How can you say that?" Mr. Conroy sounded worryingly breathless. "How— What—"

"The advertisement in *The Times* today was a message." Martin showed them the newspaper, explained the simple code, repeated himself till it sank in. "I am concerned she has followed the instructions, gone to meet him there."

"But this was published this morning! Why did you not come earlier?" Mr. Conroy demanded.

"I didn't realise its import any more than you did," Martin said, with all the patience at his command. "I came as soon as I understood it." Which was true, if incomplete. He felt strongly that the Conroys would not wish to hear that anyone else knew of their daughter's indiscretion.

"And too late," Mr. Conroy said. "She's gone, perhaps to this accursed inn. Why did you come here instead of there? Why did you not go after her at once?"

"He can't read minds, Peter, don't be absurd," Mrs. Conroy snapped. "You must go to this place. Take Martin, go now, and when you find that—that wretch she is with . . ." Her mouth worked. God knew what scenes would be passing through her mind. Her uncontrollable daughter, too young and too pampered to understand that anything could harm her, alone in an inn with an unscrupulous man.

"I have someone there already, looking for her—with her description, not her name," Martin assured them. "He is an agent I trust." That was an even less complete truth; he could not claim that he trusted Swann at all. But he was quite sure that the fellow would act shrewdly and to his own benefit, and that would certainly involve putting a stop to Miss Jennifer's escapade, since Martin had assured him that the reward would be lavish. "I am sure that if he finds her, he will act." He saw Mrs. Conroy's little sag of relief and felt a pang of compassion as he added, with reluctance, "My only fear is that she may no longer be there."

"Where else could she be?" Mrs Conroy's pitch rose on the words. "You can't be suggesting she has gone to—to—"

"She wouldn't go to some fellow's house," Mr. Conroy said flatly. "Not my Jenny. Not my little girl."

"No, sir," Martin said. "I'm concerned Troilus may be taking her to Gretna."

The words dropped into the room like stones. Mrs. Conroy's mouth opened and closed.

"We must assume he's a fortune hunter," Martin went on. "If he needs money urgently, a rich wife—"

"I won't give him a penny," Mr. Conroy said violently. "Not one. I will see him starve in the gutter first, and her with him."

"Poppycock," his wife told him. "You know very well you'll give her whatever she wants, you always do. Martin, you don't think . . . a special licence—"

"Still requires your consent. She could only marry without that in Scotland."

Mrs. Conroy nodded. "Then if she is not at this inn, I suppose we have to assume she has gone to—to marry. Or been taken by this man . . ." She rocked forward over her joined hands. "Oh, heaven help us."

"We don't know any of this for sure," Martin said. "We don't know what she's done or why. It is all guesswork, I could be wrong. Only, there is this message."

"This message, this man, my money." Mr. Conroy's jowly jaw was set. "Of course he's a fortune hunter. Oh, Jenny, *Jenny*." His voice cracked.

Mrs. Conroy looked up, face tightened in thought, then she rose with a decisive movement. "Martin. You must go after her."

"I beg your pardon?"

"You can surely catch them, get there first even, if you travel fast enough. Peter cannot." She waved a hand in the vague direction of her portly husband. Martin well knew that a coach journey at even the gentlest pace left him in agony for days. "She will listen to you, I'm sure of it. Obstinate little wretch that she is—but she has always been so fond of you. And we cannot ask anyone else, there is nobody we can trust. If word of this gets out, that she has been corresponding secretly, let alone that she has—has *eloped* . . ."

She didn't have to spell it out. The news would be ruinous for Miss Jennifer, even if the runaways were recovered. The Conroys were not in the slightest well born; their only recommendation was their wealth, and there were other rich cits, merchants and slave owners with marriageable daughters. As a scandal-stained commoner she would doubtless still snag a husband by virtue of her inheritance, but he was unlikely to be a man of character, and she would never be received in the circles of which Mrs. Conroy had dreamed.

It was a matter of utmost delicacy on which all their hopes depended, and the Conroys were confiding it to Martin. Because they trusted him with their child's secret, her life; because they knew he would do his utmost for Miss Jennifer; and because it did not occur to either of them that he was able to refuse.

Well, he could. He was no longer bound to their orders, not obliged to accede to their requests. He could not be compelled to lift a finger, far less abandon his own business to go on a wild-goose chase the length of England for the sake of the little girl he'd once dandled on his knee.

"Martin, you must," Mr. Conroy said urgently, seizing his hand. "She won't listen to anyone else, she never does. You can surely make her change her course before anything happens to her. Or if—if it is too late, she will need someone she can turn to, and who else is there she will trust in this but you or I? I am too damned old, too slow. Act for me, please. Bring our girl home."

He *could* refuse. He was under no obligation except the obligation of any person to save another from misery, if he could. The obligations of his faith, and politics, and humanity.

Martin gave an inward sigh and tightened his grip on the soft, smooth fingers he held. "I will do what I can."

Swann knocked on his door near nine o'clock that night. Martin had begun to hope that his lengthy absence meant he'd found something out, but it seemed that was not the case.

"What *did* you find?" he asked, pouring Swann a glass of port. He needed one himself, with the prospect of the next few days looming over him.

Swann grimaced, leaning back in his seat. "Well, they'd been and gone, I fear. A veiled lady meeting your description met a young gentleman in the early afternoon. He'd had his own chaise waiting and horses commanded since ten that morning. They spoke for some little while and then set off together."

"Hell's teeth. Did you get anything more? What he looks like, who he is?"

It seemed not. According to Swann, nobody had given a better description than "young gentleman," "light-brown hair," and "popinjay." Troilus had not left a name; nobody had known who he was, where he had come from, or where he had taken the young lady. Nor had anyone remembered details of his chaise.

"Nothing?" Martin demanded, incredulous. "You didn't hear a single word to identify him?"

"It's a busy inn," Swann said apologetically. "I asked everyone I could find, but no luck at all. Even the postilion who drove them on the first stage was his own. It's quite possible he chose a bustling, unfamiliar place on purpose, in order to make pursuit difficult. Or maybe he just bribes lavishly. But I could not find any clues to their destination."

"That was no damned use, then."

Swann's eyes narrowed. "You're welcome to go and ask yourself if you think you could do so more effectively. And discreetly."

Of course Martin couldn't. Swann was infinitely forgettable, born to be overlooked or dismissed. Unremarkable of height and build and manner and, most of all, complexion. A black man asking questions about the whereabouts of a genteel young white lady would stick in anyone's mind. The White Horse Cellar was one of London's busiest coaching inns, always full of travelling gentry, probably bored already and looking out for entertainment, and gossiping staff. Martin's all-too-noticeable presence could set off the very scandal that had to be contained; whereas he would wager most of the people Swann had interrogated would forget they'd been asked anything within a day.

"Very well then, we have nothing to go on," he said. "We don't even know for sure if he's taking her to Gretna. What if he's taken her to some place of his own, some house in the country?"

"Then you won't find her," Swann said bluntly. "*But*, then her parents would have grounds for an action of rape, whereas a Gretna marriage can't be challenged. He's better off marrying her by her choice than forcing the issue to leave her with none. And for her to make that choice, a trip to the border is required." He stuck his hands in his pockets. "So where does that leave matters?"

"I'm going to Gretna Green."

Swann's brows went up comically. "La, sir. Who's the fortunate fair?"

"You are," Martin said.

He hadn't precisely intended to say that. In fact, he hadn't thought about it at all. He *had* thought about a long, solitary, uncomfortable race to the border, how he'd need to command the best post-horses at every stage and be obeyed with alacrity, all the questions he'd need to ask and the cooperation he'd need to receive, and the speed at which Swann's mind worked.

And just a little bit about the way Swann had asked about earning those ten shillings and the look in his rain-coloured eyes. Which was not Martin's motive, was more like a reason to bring almost anyone else. But he needed help, and Swann already knew Miss Jennifer's secret. This way Martin would have the man under his eye, and get the assistance he needed. It made perfect sense.

Swann's expression did not suggest he'd reached the same conclusion. "What was that?"

"I am going to Gretna, in the hope of overtaking or stopping Troilus before he gets there. And you're coming with me. You can earn your pay."

"But—"

"I need someone with me, and you must see I can't bring in anyone off the street in a matter of this delicacy."

"You can't bring *me* in in a matter of delicacy," Swann objected. "I *am* off the streets. And this is a wild-goose chase if ever I heard one. You don't even know she's going to Gretna!"

"The Conroys have asked me to go, so we're going. Come on, bustle. You need to pack a bag; we'll leave at dawn tomorrow."

"I'm not doing anything of the sort!" Swann snapped. "I'm not going to Scotland, and you can't make me."

"I'm not making you. I'm *asking* you."

Swann stuttered with outrage. "You did nothing of the sort!"

"Well, consider yourself asked."

"That is not asking. And I'm not going." Swann folded his arms. "I have a business to run, the *Advertiser* to publish. I can't just hare off to Scotland."

Martin sighed. "Would five pounds change your mind?"

Swann hesitated, and then said, almost smugly, "Forty."

It was an outrageous sum. It was also Mr. Conroy's money, he had plenty to spare, and without Swann spotting the advertisement's cypher, they would have had no chance at all. "Done."

"What?" Swann looked startled, and not particularly pleased, considering the small fortune on offer.

"Forty pounds for perhaps a week of your time," Martin said. "You won't be paid like that again in a hurry. Now get on and make yourself ready to earn it."

CHAPTER THREE

Theo braced himself in the corner of the chaise, clutching the leather strap and wishing he'd asked for fifty pounds instead. If St. Vincent was spending Mr. Conroy's money so lavishly, he might as well have got his hands on more.

He was earning it just by being in this awful conveyance. It was a light travelling chaise for two passengers, owned by one of Mr. Conroy's equally wealthy but more dashing friends, and drawn by four horses, such was the urgency of their mission. They would change horses every ten or twelve miles in order to keep up the terrifying speed that was making the chaise lurch and swing as though it might topple over. The Conroys' postilion, who had driven them the first stage, had claimed they would reach the speed of fourteen miles an hour on good stretches of road. *Fourteen*! It was absurdly dangerous. Theo was beginning to feel unwell from the swaying, bounding motion. And frankly, if he was going to end up with an arse that felt as though it had been cudgelled, he could think of better ways to get there.

He could definitely think of them now. The chaise was not wide, Martin St. Vincent was a broad-built man, and they were no more than four inches apart. The jolting of this absurd conveyance could easily send Theo sprawling across his lap at any moment, a thought that sustained him for the next few miles of silence and discomfort.

"You think Gretna Green," St. Vincent said at last, his deep voice startling Theo out of the pleasurable fantasy he'd been indulging.

"If you don't, why are we in this blasted contraption?"

St. Vincent sighed. "There are other towns in Scotland where one can marry."

"Well, obviously, but Gretna is the closest to the border, is it not?"

"And the southernmost town of Scotland, yes. But the Great North Road doesn't go there directly, it runs up the east of the country. Gretna Green is to the west," St. Vincent explained, in a somewhat schoolmasterish manner. Theo adopted a look of intelligent interest. "To reach Gretna from London, one must follow the Great North Road to Boroughbridge, which lies about two-thirds of the way along our route, and then take a westerly road, travelling north through Carlisle. If our travellers stay on the Great North Road all the way, passing through Newcastle to reach the Scottish border at, say, Mordington, they will add a good forty miles to their journey, perhaps an extra day. *But*, if they do that while we go to Gretna Green, we will not stand a chance of catching them."

"Ah."

"It's some eighty miles from Gretna to where the Great North Road crosses the border, and there are half a dozen border towns where they might marry. If we take the wrong route from Boroughbridge, we'll have lost them."

"I did say this was a wild-goose chase," Theo said. "We don't know they're going to Scotland at all, and if we did, we don't know where. Are you really going to be rattled the length of the country on a whim?"

St. Vincent didn't dignify that with an answer. Theo waited a little longer, then gave a defeated sigh. "How do you know so much about flights to the border, anyway?"

"I read something on the subject recently. They have half a day's head start, but at this speed we must surely make the time up and arrive at the border first, even catch them on the way. *If* we take the right road at Boroughbridge. All depends on that."

"But that's if they continue in their private carriage," Theo pointed out. The tension in St. Vincent's voice and face suggested that he cared about the outcome of this absurd chase, and Theo felt the urge to offer a reassurance, even a false one. "If they have to go on the stage, through accident or lack of funds, say, they will be travelling at half the speed of this wingèd chariot. We should pass them well before Boroughbridge. We might wait for them there, even," he added hopefully. Cutting a hundred miles off the journey was already something he'd pay to do.

"*If* they're on the stage."

"Well, even if not, if we haven't overtaken them at Boroughbridge, we won't be far behind. Surely we'll be able to pick up their trail if we ask around, and learn which road they took. The people up there probably recognise eloping couples as soon as they step out of the carriage. I expect it's an industry of its own."

"Yes. Yes, of course." St. Vincent tipped his head back, resting it against the padded leather of the interior. "Thank you. I should doubtless have fretted over that for the next half dozen stages."

"Really?"

St. Vincent sighed. "I don't wish to go back to the Conroys without good news, and I could worry myself into a decline, sitting here with nothing to do. So I appreciate your reassurance. Your help."

"You're paying for it."

Theo wished he hadn't said that as soon as the words left his lips, and he scrabbled for some jest to soften it, but St. Vincent had already nodded and turned to look out of the window.

The journey rattled and shook on. They changed horses and again, stage after stage. The posting inns near London—*near*, indeed; they were already at Stevenage by the time they stopped for a brief nuncheon—were far too busy for anyone to remember travellers, but Theo asked his questions anyway, and felt St. Vincent's look of gratitude.

That wasn't the only look he felt, and it rapidly became clear to him why the authoritative, confident Mr. St. Vincent had wanted company. Of course Theo had known that men of colour were fewer outside London, but the significance of that fact had entirely passed him by. Now he saw. By the Stevenage stage, St. Vincent was already the only dark-skinned man present and, judging by their stares and whispers, the first most of the chawbacon patrons of the inn had seen in their lives.

St. Vincent's face was closed over as they sat with their meal. He gave no sign of noticing the gapeseeds, but he didn't speak either, keeping his attention on his food. Theo glanced around, making sure his own face showed nothing but mild interest, watching for trouble. Nobody said anything; the looks weren't even hostile, for the most part. They were simply . . . well, even *intrusive* overstated it. Just unsubtle, unrestrained by courtesy or discretion, as though St. Vincent were a spectacle for their entertainment and they were entitled to gaze their fill.

The looks weren't directed at Theo, but he felt them all the same, and spooned his stew into his mouth hastily. It was a relief, despite his aching back and arse, to get in the chaise again.

"That wasn't comfortable," he said once they were on their way.

St. Vincent didn't even ask. "No."

"And it probably won't get more comfortable as we go."

A huff of dry amusement. "Indeed not."

"I suppose you're used to it?"

St. Vincent shrugged. "I live in London. I've no need to travel."

"No." Theo considered it for a moment, feeling an unfamiliar warmth of indignation on someone else's behalf. "But why did the Conroys ask you to do this, and not a more, uh, a more unobtrusive traveller?"

"By which you mean, a whiter one." St. Vincent shrugged. "For one thing, it will not have occurred to them to consider my comfort. They have not been in the habit of that. Nor are they in the habit of leaving London, with or without me. I don't suppose they have any idea of the inconveniences of this journey."

"Oh, well. That's all right, then."

St. Vincent gave him a look he couldn't quite interpret, but went on calmly enough. "For another thing, they didn't want to tell anyone else. You must see that Miss Conroy faces ruin if word of her adventure gets out in the society in which they hope to move. They needed someone in whose loyalty and silence they could place absolute trust. Not someone who would set gossip flying around London."

Someone who would jump to their bidding, more like, leaving his own business behind to spend a miserable week rattling around over potholed roads in the arse end of nowhere. Theo suspected St. Vincent wouldn't welcome that observation. "They can't trust *my* loyalty," he pointed out instead. "Do they even know you've brought me along?"

"I'm paying well for your discretion. If you break your silence, I'll break your neck."

"Oh, very kindly said," Theo snapped. "Considering you all but pressed me into service—"

"And I don't think you are a man to destroy a woman for pleasure or profit," St. Vincent said over him.

Theo considered that from all angles, looking for sarcasm. "You don't?"

"I think you'd do a great deal for money," St. Vincent clarified. "But I would guess, probably more to yourself than to anyone else. I certainly don't think you're fool enough to try your hand at extortion, considering that I know where you live."

"Charming. Watch out or you will quite turn my head with your compliments."

"The truth, though. *Do* you intend to betray Miss Conroy's indiscretion when we return? Sell the story to the gossipmongers and ruin her for good?"

Theo flushed, but the answer was unquestionable. "No," he muttered, as though he were admitting something shameful. "There'd be no profit in it to speak of. And you'd take your fifty pounds back if I did."

"Forty."

"Can't blame a man for trying."

They exchanged smiles. St. Vincent's smile was every bit as good as Theo had suspected it might be: slow and wide, lifting his cheeks and crinkling his glinting eyes. It was the sort of smile that made a fellow feel warmed, and appreciated, and liked, even. The sort that made him want to win more smiles like that.

You're not doing this for smiles, Swann, he told himself. *You don't want his smiles.* But still he found he was grinning helplessly back.

Swann's smiles were dangerous.

Martin had already suspected it, but the conversation after the nuncheon stop had confirmed everything he feared. Swann had a sly, sideways sort of smile, insinuating, tempting; a smile that invited shared glances and secrets, and seemed to make them partners in absurdity.

Martin wanted to be partners in a great deal more than that.

He hadn't indulged with a man in over a year, since an escapade on the Sodomites' Walk in Moorfields had led to his arrest. He'd bribed the officer with an eye-watering sum to be released without charge, and decided to keep his prick to himself in the future rather than face the unspeakable consequences of using it as he wished.

He was beginning to think that had been a serious error. Between his long-controlled desires and Swann's smile, lean body, and grey, observant eyes and the inevitable closeness of this accursed journey, Martin was finding it hard not to think about ways they might spend the evening. About bending Swann—Theodore, his name was—over a bedstead, or putting him on hands and knees. About how he would push and wriggle and demand. Martin was quite sure he'd be demanding.

Which was neither here nor there. It was too dangerous. It was *all* dangerous: Swann's smile and Martin's rogue thoughts and this closeness in a jolting carriage, and the fact that the more he told himself not to be a fool, the more he wanted to be one.

That thing Swann had said. *What else will you have from me for your money?* If ten shillings had been enough to buy him Swann's arse, God knew what forty pounds would pay for.

No amount would buy the light in his eyes when he'd really smiled, when it had been spontaneous and gleeful and shared. But that sort of thing was the most dangerous of all. That was where a man or woman became a fool and put everything to hazard for the sake of a fantasy. Like Miss Jennifer, throwing away her future and her reputation for the thrill of a romance with a man she didn't even know.

Christ in heaven, he hoped she was well. Please God Troilus was wooing her gently. Please God she had not been compromised against her will. The thought went some way to quelling his own desires for his travelling partner.

They talked idly as the coach rolled and bounced them through the afternoon. There was nothing else to do.

"How is it that you publish your newspaper?" Martin asked at one point. "Why matrimonial advertisements, of all things?"

Swann shrugged. "Profitable."

"Is that all?"

"What else is there? If you're asking whether I am a matchmaker by nature . . ."

"It seems to me there are other things to advertise."

"None of which I know about. Not that I know a great deal about matrimony, truth be told. But matrimonial publications speak to a wide audience, and I have no trouble filling my pages. A man has to live somehow."

"It's not what you'd have chosen?" Martin asked curiously.

"Eh." It seemed as though Swann might leave it there, but after a few minutes he said, "My parents destined me to be a curate."

"You?" Martin said with, he realised too late, rather more incredulity than was quite polite.

"Yes, well. They had a number of hopes for me which I did not fulfil. And made great efforts to help me achieve them, but . . . Suffice to say, I found myself at twenty with no degree, no prospects, and a deal of disgrace. I had to— Well, I shan't bore you with the sordid details."

Martin turned to look at him. Swann had on a hard smile, shaped to show how little he cared.

"I was left with debts to pay and a regrettable need to eat. And since my family were unable or unwilling to assist me further, and I had nothing to offer any employer but some insincerely held knowledge of theology, I struck out on my own. I run the *Advertiser*, I make a certain amount by my writing, I live."

He sounded startlingly unenthusiastic about that last. Martin frowned. "Have you reconciled to your parents?"

"No. Perhaps we might have, one day, but it's too late for that. Typhus."

"I'm sorry to hear it."

Swann gave another of those one-shouldered shrugs. "Well."

"I'm sorry," Martin said again. "It is not easy to make one's own way, or to redress mistakes. I should not have been so scornful when we met."

"If I could not tolerate the scorn of others, I should be a very unhappy man."

The bareness of that took Martin's breath away. He sat for a moment, absorbing it, and said at last, "That is not . . . Why should you tolerate it?"

"I earned it. My parents were not wealthy, and they sacrificed more than I realised to give me the future I threw away." His voice was raw with old bitterness. Martin realised he was reaching out a hand to give a comforting touch, pulled it back.

"And as for the *Advertiser*, of course everyone mocks those fool enough to admit their hopes in public," Swann went on. "After all, what is more absurd than a lonely woman hoping for a husband, or a man who cannot command a wife for himself? Are those not laughable spectacles? I make my money from hopes and dreams laid bare, and those are too important, too revealing, to be treated with anything except scorn."

The chaise lurched sideways, righted itself, bowled on.

"I see what you mean, I think," Martin said. "The poets and playwrights and novelists write about love, and we devour it, but the actual business of matrimony—"

"*Is* a business," Swann completed. "And to be unbusinesslike is to be ridiculous, or ruined. Look at Miss Conroy, becoming soiled goods in the marketplace by following her heart, instead of gaining the world's approval by exchanging her cu—her person for a title."

Martin shifted slightly. "You cannot think a man who runs away with a young lady means well by her."

"I wonder if anyone does," Swann said. "Look at us all in this affair. The Conroys want to offer their daughter in exchange for a title, and Troilus, like all her respectable suitors, wants her money, and she wants to pursue her foolish ideas of pleasure without regard for the future or her parents' wish, and I want fifty pounds—"

"Forty."

"And what do you want?" Swann asked. "What do you get from this? Are you here in this damned uncomfortable contraption, leaving your own business untended for a week or more, simply because you are a chivalrous knight riding to the rescue? Why are you dancing to the Conroys' tune?"

Martin couldn't answer that for a moment. He stared out of the little window, trying to formulate words, and realised the chaise wheels were grinding more slowly under them.

"We're at a staging post," he said, and offered nothing else.

Southoe was worse than Stevenage. There were only two horses to be had, which would slow their pace, and the ostler examined the coins Martin handed over, with a suspicious eye that made him set his teeth. The postilion whispered to his replacement as they changed the horses—about what, Martin could not tell, but they glanced at him, and a couple of barmaids and drinkers drifted outside to take a look as he walked around the yard stretching his sore legs.

He hated this. Hated travelling outside London, hated being a novelty. He wanted to ask them what the devil they were looking at.

Doing no harm, he told himself over again. *Just curious.* As the men who followed him to the jakes were doubtless just curious to get a look at his privy parts. That also was nothing new.

He walked back to the inn yard, keeping his breathing calm and even. Swann was there, talking to an ostler with what looked to Martin like a great deal too much friendliness. He raised a hand, and Swann came across to meet him, dodging a pile of dung.

"Well?" Martin said, and regretted his curtness at once. This wasn't Swann's fault.

"Well, we've their scent. That fellow told me. A young lady, veiled, and a gentleman escorting her. Flash look, light-brown hair, and he cursed the men for not changing the horses quickly enough. They're travelling— Are you all right?"

"Very well." Martin had to listen; this was important. This was what they were here for. "Go on, please."

"They're travelling in a private coach and evidently at speed. It seems the postilion complained that he'd been shouted at to spring the horses the whole way. And the gentleman didn't tip well."

"Which is to say he may be short of money."

"Certainly if I were a runaway and plump in the pocket, I'd pay for silence," Swann said. "But he may simply be a grasping skinflint, hard to say. The postilion who drove them has gone back London-wards already."

"How far ahead are they?"

"They passed through at around noon."

Martin glanced up; it was six o'clock now. "So we have six hours yet to make up. We need to press on while the light lasts. They may do the same, and we cannot afford to lose the time."

Swann made a face. "Troilus is travelling with a lady. He may give her tender parts more consideration than you're giving mine."

"Your tender parts are at the forefront of my mind," Martin said. It was intended to be sarcasm, but as the words emerged they sounded more like regrettable accuracy.

"That much is obvious," Swann told him, leaving him quite without retort. "Come on, the hell-trap awaits."

They didn't speak for a while after the chaise jolted off, both settling onto the hard seats that Martin's arse was coming to hate. Since he was brutally uncomfortable anyway, he made himself ask the question he had wanted to avoid.

"Swann. Did you happen to enquire if the young lady was travelling with a maidservant, or other attendant?"

Swann grimaced. "I didn't have to. The ostler volunteered that she was not."

"Hell's teeth."

"It was one of the reasons they were memorable. And this will be their second night."

Martin shut his eyes briefly. "I know."

"Even if we catch them before the wedding—"

"I know."

"That will be his intent, of course. Make it impossible for her not to marry him."

"I know."

"I'm not sure why you dragged me on this farrago of a journey if you know everything already."

Martin shot him a glance. "Tender parts paining you?"

"Oh, be quiet." Swann shifted resentfully in his seat.

"You're right, of course," Martin said after a while. "But the situation still may be salvageable. At least we can try."

"Are you fond of her?" Swann asked. "Miss Conroy?"

"Fond?" Martin repeated. "Uh . . . I have known her since her birth. She's lively. Laughs a great deal. Strong-willed, overindulged, but, yes, I'm fond of her. I shouldn't wish to see her suffer."

"Is that why you're dragging yourself and me through the dunghills of England? Your fondness for her?"

"You don't give up easily, do you?" It was well past six in the evening, and they had at least another two hours in the coach, maybe even three, if they were to manage another two stages before dark. Martin wanted a pint of ale, and a seat that didn't move, and a hot meal, and he wanted . . . "Why does it matter?"

"Curiosity." Swann hesitated, and then went on, "As I said, this is no small task you're about. I wondered what the Conroys have done to deserve such friendship."

Friendship. Martin stared out of the dirty little window, at the monotonous green of fields, feeling his cravat a constriction about his neck. "I spent my childhood in their household."

"Ah."

Swann understood what that meant, Martin was sure he did, but he said it anyway. "As a slave. Household slave. I wore a silver collar, engraved with their name." He didn't look around; he didn't want to see Swann's expression. "They fed me well, and gave me an education—reading, writing, mathematics. My tasks were not onerous. I was never beaten except in the normal way of mischievous children. I was always well treated, *always*, and when I was eighteen they freed me with a gift of money to set up for myself. And Mr. Conroy presented me with the, uh, the collar. As a memento."

"Christ alive," Swann said. "I wish you'd rammed it back in his teeth."

Martin looked round then, and the breath he heard himself give sounded like a sob in his own ears. "So do I," he said harshly. "And I shouldn't. They were the best possible masters—"

"Bloody end to me," Swann muttered, the oath slurred into something like *enemy*. "Was there much competition for that title?"

"Yes," Martin said. "Mr. Conroy has sugarcane plantations. Do you know about those? He could have shipped me out there when I grew, sold me, he could have— Do you have any idea what he could have done? What the law permits him to do?"

"I— Some. Yes."

"I was always well treated," Martin said again. "I could so easily not have been. I know how my life might have played out. There was a time, during the revolution in France, when Mr. Conroy's business went through difficulties, and it seemed he might find it necessary to sell me—"

"Sweet King Jesus."

"But he didn't. Instead I was kept in the household, and freed on such generous terms that I have been able to prosper ever since, and how can I resent that?"

"That sounds to me the kind of generosity that could kill a man."

Martin let his head thud back against the leather rest. "It is. It sticks in my throat like thistles, it *chokes* me." His hand was at his throat, he realised, that old habitual gesture. He let it drop and repeated, quietly, "It chokes me."

Swann bit his lip. "You know, speaking as a trained theologian and potential parson, I don't think you have to be thankful that someone refrained from doing something terrible to you. You could break my neck now, I'm sure, and I am not remotely grateful that you aren't doing so."

"But I should hang if I broke your neck," Martin said. "Breaking necks is not a legal trade that earns men knighthoods for their success. I don't lose profit by *not* breaking your neck. Do you know how much the Conroys gave me as a gift? A hundred pounds. That was Mr. Conroy's estimate of what I would fetch at the auction block."

"Christ Jesus *fuck*," Swann said. "Fuck them both and their brat. Let's leave her to her sluttery and go home."

Martin pressed his lips together to prevent something. A laugh, or not. "Is that how you'd have written your sermons, Reverend Swann?"

"Theo, for God's sake." He exhaled hard. "And, very well. Let us grant that a man is entitled to copulate with his wife. Should she give thanks, every time she is not in the mood to oblige him, that he does not throw her down and force her to it? Should she consider him a good husband merely for that restraint?"

"I know," Martin said, more harshly than he meant. "You don't need to tell me what I should think. I *know*."

Theo held up a hand in apology. "I beg your pardon. I, uh, feel strongly about gratitude. Forced gratitude, I mean, the kind piled on your debt as added interest. To be ground underfoot and then told to be thankful the foot was not heavier—I hate it. I expect you hate it a great deal worse than I." He paused, thinking. "And I have heard about plantations and the things that are done there. If that might have been my lot in life, I would have been damned happy to avoid it too."

"That was never in question for you," Martin said. "It was for me. I am angry, believe me. I am more angry than you can imagine, and I will always be angry, but I am also very glad that was not my life. And that was all in the Conroys' hands, always." Obligation and resentment and guilty relief, ever there, knotted together.

"So this pays them back," Theo said. "Is that it? If you retrieve Miss Conroy, a life for a life?"

Martin looked blankly forward. It had not occurred to him to think of this mission in those terms. In the end, he'd done what was asked because he still loved the laughing little girl who had climbed on his lap demanding stories. "I doubt they will see it so."

"I don't give a hound's tits what they think. What do *you* think?"

Martin considered it. He would, undeniably, have rendered the Conroys a service—a *favour*—that ought to earn their gratitude in full measure. But a life for a life? "Perhaps."

Theo exhaled hard, ruffling his lips, but said no more.

Martin didn't speak either. He had never said so much in his life, and he wasn't sure why he had let it all spill out at this time, to this man. Because he was exhausted by silence? Because Theo was so very unimportant? Because he'd asked, when nobody else had?

Whatever the reason, it was more than Martin had ever said, because he could not usually bring himself to complain of his lot. He had been, without question, the best treated of any slave or even servant of his acquaintance, and was now prospering beyond what many in London, black or white, could dream of. So he contributed what he could to the Stingo's coffers for the needy poor, helped his fellows set up their own shops and coffeehouses in their own little part of London, and tried endlessly to work away the corrosive guilt at his undeserved good fortune.

Good fortune, to be stolen from your home and shipped across the seas. But as Mr. Conroy had once advised him, in such firm yet kindly tones, otherwise he would have spent his life breaking his back and hands in the sugarcane fields, under the whip. *You should remember how lucky you are*, the Conroys had often said. And that was wrong, filthily wrong, but his youth had been haunted by the spectres of how much worse it might have been, of feeling glad it was not worse for himself and ashamed to compare his lot with that of others. He had spent his life twisting in the meshes of that net.

The pain in his palms made him realise that his hands were fisted, nails digging in. He forced himself to relax them.

Theo was watching him.

"I don't want your pity," Martin said, almost a snarl.

"You won't get it," Theo said. "I reserve sentiments of pity entirely for myself."

Martin couldn't help a laugh.

Theo smiled back, then it faded a little. "Uh," he said. "Your family . . .?"

"I don't know. I was perhaps four when I was brought to England. A gift from a Dutch friend of theirs who had a plantation on the island of St. Vincent. I don't remember anything before the ship."

"What a pretty token. Some people would have brought flowers. What did you do with the collar?"

"Why?"

Theo shrugged. "I was trying to think what I would do with such a gift, and I cannot. Keep it, throw it away, sell it and spend the proceeds on drink?"

"I sold it to a jeweller, and used what I got for it to buy a girl at auction. Peggy, my housekeeper."

"Oh," Theo said slowly. "Yes, of course. Did that help?"

"In its way. Although she was a thorough-going domestic affliction at first. The scourge of my crockery." He found he was smiling again, the knot in his chest a little looser. Peggy, just twelve when he'd bought and freed her, had anchored his angry, directionless bewilderment after his emancipation, giving him a reason to think twice, to stay calm, to succeed.

"It's so hard to get good staff," Theo agreed. "I manage my household by not having one, and curling up in a corner of my office like a stray dog." He said it in the tones of a joke, and Martin laughed accordingly, but he had seen the couch and blankets under piles of paper, and it struck him to wonder how Theo spent the money he must surely make.

Not his business. He let out a long breath, consciously relaxing his shoulders. "Thank you."

Theo looked a little startled. "For what?"

"Listening, I suppose." Listening, and the flare of angry defence, and the expression in his eyes that spoke of sympathy rather than pity. Martin would never ask for those things, but they were undeniably warming to have. "I don't talk about it a great deal. I daresay you're sorry you asked," he added, with an effort at lightness.

"No," Theo said. "So this is what success in our quest means to you, then? More than Miss Conroy's well-being?"

"That's my first concern," Martin said, a little puzzled that he'd returned to the question. "But I can't deny I want to succeed for—let's say, my own satisfaction."

"To do the Conroys a favour for which they will have to be grateful. Right," Theo said. "Right. Well, I suppose we'd better press on."

CHAPTER FOUR

By the time they stopped for the night, outside Newark-on-Trent, Theo had decided that the only people on earth he despised more than the Conroy family were, firstly, the man who called himself Troilus, and secondly, the whoreson damned fool who had invented the very idea of chaises. Everything hurt, from the soles of his feet to the crown of his head.

He'd ordered the horses at the previous stage, where they could and probably should have stopped for the night. He'd done it without consultation, in the teeth of his own wishes, and he wasn't entirely sure why.

The immediate reason was obvious: he hadn't wanted to make Martin ask him to do it. But beyond that . . . It was because he wanted to make Martin feel that he was on his side, he told himself, but he had a sinking suspicion that wasn't true.

The fact was, he wanted to *be* on Martin's side, which was a different thing entirely. He wanted to be helping him, he wanted them to be working together, he wanted that shared understanding. He wanted to help Martin find the girl and return her to her home virgo intacta, and he wanted Martin to let go a little of his unhappiness when he did it. He wanted more of those smiles.

He was a mutton-headed gaby, and he needed to keep an eye on his own interests, and not confuse them with his interest in the fit of Martin's breeches, either. Martin needed to catch their fugitives; Theo did not, and he was a clodpole to sacrifice his arse on the altar of Miss Conroy's virginity, he thought as he walked, sore and stiff-legged, into the Royal Oak.

As it was, they were late arrivals. Naturally, everyone looked around as they walked in. Naturally, everyone kept looking at Martin.

Theo had never wanted to be a big man, except on the few occasions he'd had his scrawny arse well booted, usually because of his too-ready mouth. He wished that he could loom intimidatingly now, ask the lot of them what the devil they were staring at. Instead he ignored the gawping rustic clowns as only a Londoner could ignore people, and stalked, as best he could with his aching thighs, to the bar.

"Two ales and whatever you have hot to eat," he told the landlord. "And we'll need beds for the night."

The landlord flickered a look over Theo's shoulder, at his companion. "Blackamoor's with you, is he?"

Theo made his best effort to deliver the sort of freezing glare he'd frequently received from his tutors. "Mr. St. Vincent and I are on urgent business. We've no time to lose, so we'll need to leave at first light. We'd like—" He rephrased that. "You'll make sure we're roused before dawn with the horses ready to depart at first light." He let the man open his mouth before adding, "So we'll settle with you for all that this evening, and here's something more for the trouble we'll be putting you to. Oh, and we'll dine in a private parlour," he added, as though he commanded such things daily.

Money was a marvellous thing. The colour of the Conroys' coin quite outweighed the colour of his companion's skin, and they were shortly seated in a little room, small and snug, each with a mug of good ale, and a little of the tension was fading from Martin's face. Theo had come to the firm conclusion that if the Conroys were putting them through this, they could damned well pay for it.

Martin was obviously thinking along similar lines, if going in a different direction, because he said, "You're making very free with the funds."

"Well, we need the fools here willing to bestir themselves in the morning. And I for one want a bit of comfort if we're to keep that pace up. My arse feels like a blacksmith's anvil with the pounding it's taken."

Martin's lips parted slightly, as though he were about to make a retort in kind, and then snapped shut. Theo chalked that one up to himself with a little satisfaction.

"I just hope they've food in the house," Martin said instead. "If they can make us something edible, I'll be a contented man."

"I'll eat anything they put in front of me. Maybe even the plate."

As it proved, he didn't have to devour the china. The host served them himself, with great hunks of a well-cooked ham, eggs, new bread, and a dish of peas, all excellent. Theo hadn't eaten anything so fresh since he'd moved to London, and had not had peas like this since he'd picked them himself at home. He wolfed about half his plateful down before slowing to savour the rest, and glanced up to see Martin's grin. "What are you looking at?"

"Good to see a man enjoy his food."

"Well, if I must be dragged to the country, I might as well enjoy the benefits."

"Wise." Martin was clearing his own plate with alacrity. Theo surrendered the remaining bread to him, as the bigger man, but made sure he snagged another spoonful of peas for himself.

Bodily needs—or those particular ones, at least—met, he wiped his lips and leaned back in his chair. Martin was still eating, and Theo watched him while his attention was on his food, watched the movement of his throat and jaw, and let his imagination play.

It was ten o'clock by the time they'd both finished their meal. Each had ordered a second mug of ale as they ate. Theo sipped at his, eyes on Martin over the rim of the tankard as he pored over the map the landlord had been induced to lend.

"We've covered something close to a hundred and twenty miles, I think," Martin said.

"In a single day," Theo said, incredulous. "Great heavens. No wonder my arse hurts."

"Stop telling me about your arse."

"I wouldn't tell you if you didn't care."

"I do not care!"

"I'm sure you do," Theo said. "Deep down, under that gruff exterior, beats a heart of gold with an urgent concern for the condition of my arse."

"It does not. Stop playing the fool." Martin kept his eyes on the map, lips clamped together, with an expression of serious concentration that might have fooled a particularly unobservant child. "Perhaps eighty miles to Boroughbridge, and they six hours ahead. Five if they stopped sooner than we. I don't think we'll catch them tomorrow."

"But we'll surely find their trail there." Mine host and the ostlers of the Royal Oak had not seen the fugitives, but Newark was a sizeable town, with plenty of coaching inns. It would be an effort Theo was disinclined to make to walk round them all, asking whether their quarry had passed through. "Though we may need to stop a little while in Boroughbridge to be sure we discover which route they take."

"If they stay on the Great North Road we'll have them before the border," Martin said, as if reassuring himself. "Surely."

"We'll catch them yet, I'm sure of it," Theo said. "Come on, let's retire. We need the early start."

They had a shared room, two beds. Theo had requested that. His reason, ready to be offered if asked for, was that he'd flashed around their money in a strange place and who knew what uncivilised tricks rustics got up to with wealthy travellers? Safety in numbers, he'd have said.

Martin didn't ask, though. Didn't ask, didn't comment, didn't look while Theo changed into his nightshirt. That was probably because he was a decent man with morals who knew right from wrong.

Theo looked. He watched Martin pull his white shirt over his head, baring his deep chest, a rich glinting brown in the candlelight. Watched his smooth back as he poured water from the ewer and splashed his face and neck, rubbed his arms and chest, leaving glistening streaks and droplets running down his back like tears.

He was still watching, unable to do anything else, when Martin turned and their eyes met.

They stared at each other. Theo sitting in bed in his nightshirt, caught in the act, knowing damned well that his arousal was visibly tenting the linen. Martin, stripped to the waist, standing a few feet away.

There had to be something Theo could say that would bring him those few steps closer, over whatever line of uncertainty or belief or convention lay in his way. Something that would make it quite clear what Theo wanted, what they both wanted.

Or perhaps there wasn't. Christ, perhaps he'd misread incomprehension or tolerance of his nonsense, and now he'd pushed too far and he was about to find himself abandoned here, thrown out, beaten bloody—

Martin swallowed, once, throat working so that the little black pinprick mark moved up and down. That was his only movement. He didn't step away or cover himself, and Theo knew with a shudder of relief for more than the safety of his person that he hadn't been wrong.

"When you said you didn't want to hear any more about my arse," he began.

"Oh, for—"

"It's *very* sore." He offered a ludicrously wide-eyed look that won him a splutter of laughter. "You could at least offer me a rubdown."

Martin shut his eyes. "Theo . . ."

"We're in the middle of nowhere. We needn't stop here again. And if I'm going to have a sore arse tomorrow anyway—"

"For God's sake!" Martin jerked his head around, though there had been no sound from the hallway and the door was shut and bolted.

Theo stretched out in the bed, not bothering to pull down the hem of his nightshirt as it rode up. "There's nobody here but you and me, and if we're quiet, it'll stay that way."

"You're presuming a great deal." Martin's voice was level, but his eyes had moved down from Theo's face, and his lips were slightly parted.

"I'm very presumptuous." Theo slid a hand down himself, pulling the loose linen tight over his chest, then travelling further, down to his own bare thigh, and then up again, fingers delving under the nightshirt. Martin swallowed again. "I presume you might want to come over here and let me have a suck of you, to start with." He edged the nightshirt up, over his hips, so the cloth bunched against his cockstand.

"God's truth," Martin said under his breath, and came forward with, Theo noted, all the difficulties attendant on breeches that weren't designed to hold what looked like an impressively rampant prick. He stopped by the edge of the bed, looking down. "Just . . . why?"

"Why what? Why do I want to suck you?" Theo looked him up and down, taking his time. It wasn't a hardship. "How would I not?"

"This is not— I don't wish to insult you," Martin said with care, "but this is not what I am paying you for, nor what you're obliged to provide."

Theo narrowed his eyes. "Sweetling, if you were paying me for this, it would *definitely* be fifty guineas."

Martin took that in for a second, and then he was on the bed, kneeling across and over Theo, legs to each side and hands bracketing his face. Theo stared up into those dark eyes, copper-flecked in the candlelight, feeling his breath come short.

"Do you kiss?" Martin asked, so low it was almost hard to hear.

That wasn't a question that often arose for Theo. When he did use his mouth, it was more tongue-fucking than kissing. He'd never kissed in the way that Miss Conroy had doubtless imagined her elopement would bring, the way that Adelina and his other heroines might expect to be kissed by their bland heroes in the last chapters of his books. The way that heroes kissed in his head, sometimes, in the romances he could never write or publish.

He doubted Martin would kiss him that way either, but he was open to whatever was on offer. "Why not?" he said, and Martin's mouth came down on his.

He was taller than Theo and much more powerfully built, but his touch was so light, so careful. Almost chaste, except his full lips were just a little way apart. Theo would have lunged, or thrust with his tongue, hurried matters up a little, but he was on his back with Martin above him, braced on his elbows and dipping his head, and it was easier simply to let him set the pace.

Easier. Sweeter. Frightening. Because Martin was kissing him so very gently, as if this were a wooing, not just the fuck Theo wanted. As if he were making love, as if Theo was worth making love to.

Martin's tongue teased his lips, and Theo opened to him. *Why don't you get on with it*, he should have said, or *I'd rather a cock than a kiss, thank you*, but he didn't. Instead he kissed Martin back, not sure what he was doing, shutting his eyes against the tenderness of it as their lips moved together, and knew a sense of profound relief when Martin lowered his body a little, bringing that solid weight and the bulge of a hard cock against his thigh. That was what he understood, and wanted, and could deal with.

He kissed Martin a little harder, squirming as he did it, felt the response at once. Martin's mouth pressed closer, his tongue becoming less exploratory and more possessive. Theo ground up against him, heard a grunt, did it again, tongues plunging and tangling now. He got his hands round Martin's solid arse and grabbed.

"Christ," Martin gasped into his mouth, and thrust against him in a way that made everything between ribs and knees ache in anticipation. Theo thrust back, mimicking the motion, and then they were rutting against each other, with Theo's nightshirt rumpled and tangled between them, his bare prick between Martin's clothed thighs.

"You need those breeches off," Theo told him. "And then you need to do something with that cockstand, or I'll do it for you."

Martin had to roll off the bed to get himself stripped, while Theo discarded his nightshirt. He expected Martin to pounce back on him, but he didn't. He stood bare by the side of the bed, looking down, and Theo looked up at his corded thighs and broad, almost hairless chest with a sudden lump in his throat for his own pallid insignificance.

No wonder Martin hadn't leapt at the opportunity to have a stoop-shouldered narrow-chested inky-fingered grubbing wordsmith in his bed. If Theo had a body like that, he'd spend all day admiring himself in the looking glass. *And* he'd make damned sure he partnered it with the kind of body he deserved.

Well, he might not have that body, but he had a mouth, and the skills to use it. He sat up, swung his legs off the bed, and reached out to the prick so conveniently close to his lips.

Martin made a strangled sound. Theo studied the view: the interplay of muscle, sinew, and bone, curls of black hair, a stand made to be relished. It was a little darker than the rest of him; flushed with blood, Theo supposed. He splayed his hands over Martin's thighs, skin to skin, leaned forward, and took him in his mouth.

Martin's hands closed gently on Theo's shoulders. Theo wanted less of the gentleness. He gave it just a moment, working his tongue round the smooth skin and firm flesh, accustoming himself to Martin's smell and taste and feel, and then he busied himself. Sliding his lips down, opening his throat, taking Martin deep in a long, smooth movement that filled his mouth and senses, and had Martin's fingers digging into his shoulders. He did it again, and again, faster, first pleasuring and then fucking him with his mouth, sliding his hands between Martin's legs and then up and down the crease of his firm arse until finally the man seemed to grasp the delicate hint he was offering.

"Theo." Hands pushing against his shoulders. He pulled back, letting the saliva-wet prick rest in his open mouth. He knew just how provocative that looked, and he saw the tremor as Martin registered it. "Dear God. Get on the bed."

Theo sprawled back, grasping one of Martin's hands as he went and tugging, so that Martin ended up over him once again. He dipped down to take Theo's mouth—he would taste himself there—and as he did it his hand closed on Theo's stand. Theo thrust up into the grip, opened his mouth to the plundering, and clawed his need into Martin's broad, smooth back.

"You," Martin gasped. "Hell's teeth. Theo. I want . . ."

"Then take it, blast you." Theo lunged upward to get his mouth to Martin's neck, propping himself with an awkwardly angled hand.

"Oil. Or grease."

Theo didn't have any such thing with him, and the thought of nipping downstairs to beg a pat of butter from the kitchen was not in the least appealing. Perhaps they might think nothing of such an odd request, but he had no intention of rousing suspicion. A country gaol cell would be the least of their troubles if they were caught.

"I've none. Come here and I'll wet it for you."

"I'm not doing this with spit," Martin said flatly. "Damned if I'm listening to you bitch about your arse all tomorrow as well."

"Oh, get on, will you? I've done worse."

Martin let go his cock and shoved him down onto the bed, making Theo gasp with the sudden movement. Hand heavy on his shoulder, prick rubbing gently against his. He whimpered.

"You are not going to share a bed with me and walk away saying, 'I've done worse.'" Martin's voice was slightly ragged, and his eyes were fixed on Theo's with disturbing intensity. "That is not how I fuck."

Theo would wager it wasn't, and the thought made him all the more urgent to find out firsthand. "I don't mind. If you go gently— Mph." That was Martin's mouth, cutting him off, his hand closing around both lengths. Theo attempted to make a noise of objection, but it came out sounding embarrassingly like capitulation.

Martin sat up after a little, right up, planting his hands on Theo's shoulders and looking down. "I want to give you something to complain about tomorrow," he said, somewhat hoarsely. "Believe me. But, uh, I've experience of this—"

"You think I don't?"

"Of it not going well," Martin said. "I use oil."

It didn't sound as though he would negotiate. Theo gave a snarl of frustration. "I should have packed something. I bloody knew I should."

"Oh, did you?"

Theo hooked a hand round Martin's prick. "Be honest. This has been waiting for me for days. Begging, probably."

"I am going to stop that mouth for you," Martin said, and moved forward with intent. Theo slid down the bed to assist, and then Martin was in his mouth again, and this time Martin was leading. He drove down, steady but not gentle now, fucking into Theo's mouth, filling his throat. Theo sucked him in a frenzy of need, writhing under him, desperate for it all now. Martin's spend, his desire, the proof that Theo was wanted even just for half an hour.

"Christ, I'm going to—" Martin tried to pull back, just a little; Theo dug his fingers into Martin's arse and urged him down, his toes curling into the bedclothes with tension as the other man stiffened, reached his peak, and spent hard, right down Theo's throat.

They were still for a moment, Martin with head bowed, breathing hard; Theo relishing the sharp-sweet taste of him before he slowly, deliberately swallowed and set about licking Martin's piece clean.

"Dear God." Martin's voice rasped. "If I'd thought . . . I *did* think."

Theo had to wriggle up a bit to get his mouth free. "What did you think?"

Martin looked at him, as if weighing something up. "I hope I don't offend you if I say, I thought you'd fuck like a tomcat."

"You don't offend me," Theo said. "Not to speak of."

"No, I don't think I do." Martin's hand moved back, closing on Theo's rigid stand. "Dear heaven, I want to know what you'll be like with my prick in you. What you'll feel like, what you'll look like. You're the kind who can't stop moving, aren't you?"

Theo's breath was coming short. "You could find out. You could fuck me now—"

"After that? Believe me, I could not, for a while yet," Martin said, with a fleeting grin. "But . . ." He shifted down the bed, then took hold of Theo's stand again and began to work it, sliding his thumb over the wet, slippery head in a way that made Theo's toes curl. "Is that just from having me in your mouth?"

"What else d'you think I've been doing?"

"You don't give an inch, do you?"

"I just took at least eight," Theo pointed out.

"And loved it." Martin's hand was moving faster. "And wanted more. Wanton little piece, aren't you?"

Theo groaned agreement, hips jerking, watching Martin watching him. He did want more, but Martin's other hand was stroking and teasing now, pushing his legs apart and roaming between as if . . .

As if he wanted to know Theo. As if he wanted his pleasure. As if he cared, because the intent, careful, almost joyful expression on his face was that of a man who cared.

Theo bit down hard on his own lip and shut his eyes so that he didn't have to see.

CHAPTER FIVE

The next day, Martin had a headache.

That wasn't surprising; they'd fucked far too late into the night. It was Theo's fault for being so damned . . . whatever it was that he was; Martin wasn't even sure. He only knew that he hadn't wanted to disentangle himself from that sinewy, twisty body, and by the time he'd been ready to move, Theo had been ready for another bout, and it would have been rude to decline. He'd ended up driving between Theo's tight-clamped thighs, with his companion whispering the most obscene encouragement in his ears, and spending all over him. Theo had wiped it up with a hand and deliberately licked the seed from his ink-blackened fingers. It was a sight Martin thought he'd probably take to his grave.

So they'd heard the chimes at midnight, and been roused by a resentful-looking chambermaid at half past four, and Martin's head was throbbing even after a cup of strong coffee. Theo looked in similar plight, skin somewhat greyish, attempting to find a position in which he might doze without falling off the seat of the chaise. Martin wished him luck with that.

What *was* it about him?

Proximity, perhaps. A willing man; something to do on this dreadful journey, at once endlessly tedious and nail-chewingly tense. They were bored, Martin was strung as tight as a fiddle, and they both inclined to men. No more explanation needed.

Except that wasn't true, or sufficient. Martin had spoken of things that he never spoke of, and Theo had understood. Better than that, he'd listened when he didn't understand. That was new. That had soothed something, just a little.

He'd *listened*. He'd been angry, too, for Martin. Martin was used to being angry, but he was the fortunate one. He couldn't ask people to be angry for him when there were so many others in so much worse case. He didn't ask for pity, because he didn't need or deserve it. Or want it, either. Pity was for children, and he was very weary of being treated as a child.

He had wondered last night, just for a moment, if Theo might be offering himself out of pity. That had not been an appealing prospect, any more than the other thoughts that whispered behind it: *Because of the money. Because you're a novelty. Because he wants to tell his friends what a man of colour's like.*

He'd been a fool to think it. Theo had wanted to fuck Martin because he liked to fuck, as simple as that. There had been no other motives, and no sentiment either. Just two people enjoying themselves and each other.

Except for those moments—seconds—when something raw had crossed Theo's face. Martin had seen it, but the fleeting expressions had come and gone so quickly, and always been followed by a surge of movement that left his enthusiasm in no doubt. Still, their memory caught at him.

Maybe, if he bought oil for tonight, he'd find out more.

Thoughts of that kept his drifting mind occupied while the headache ebbed. They took time for more coffee at the next stage, since it was still only six in the morning. That also meant that they were able to secure four horses, fresh after a night's rest, and made excellent time, covering the twelve miles to Retford in just fifty minutes, even if Martin felt as though his teeth had been jolted out of his head. The third stage was longer, and it was half past eight when they finally stopped at the Hare and Tortoise inn, outside Rossington.

"I need breakfast," Theo said as they lowered themselves down the steps of the chaise. It was the first sentence he'd managed since they'd woken.

"Breakfast, more coffee," Martin agreed, taking a look around. The air was fresh here, so far from London's festering smells, and not yet heated and dusty. The red-brick inn seemed neat and clean, and he could smell bacon frying. Next to him, Theo gave a small whimper.

"You order," Martin said, with a gentle push between Theo's shoulder blades. He stumbled off to the door while Martin gave the ostlers their instructions, choosing to believe their wide-eyed expressions were because the accents up here were so thick that it was becoming a challenge to make the words out. A couple of shillings seemed to aid their comprehension, and he even got a "Yes, sir" from the brighter looking of them.

Inside the inn, Theo was doing a manful job of crawling into the coffeepot. Martin joined him at the table, poured himself a cup of what remained and, realising that conversation would be in short supply for a while yet, took out his book. He'd brought a couple, since he hadn't known that the pace of the carriage would make reading quite impossible, or that his nights might offer other entertainment.

He'd read a few pages before he became aware that Theo was watching him with a stunned expression.

"What is it?"

"Uh . . . what are you reading?"

"Just a novel."

"A novel," Theo repeated.

"A novel, yes. Do you not read novels?"

"Yes. Yes, I do. Why are you reading that one?"

Martin closed the book and turned it around. It was a cheap edition, with no name or title printed on the binding. "How do you know what I'm reading?"

Theo blinked. "What *are* you reading?"

He was very clearly not at his best in the mornings. Martin sighed. "It's a romance, called *Melusina*. There's a young lady in peril from a villainous uncle who wants to keep her locked away until she's old enough to be married for her money— Ah, excellent," he added as the serving girl approached carrying two huge trenchers laden with enough sausage and bacon to fortify a small army.

The food seemed to revive Theo. He washed down his third rasher with a swig of coffee from the second pot, which Martin had thought it judicious to order, and asked, "Did you command the horses?"

"I did. We've four again."

"Good. Good." Theo concentrated on carving off a chunk of excellent sausage. "Uh, are you enjoying it? Your book?" he added, into his plate.

"Reasonably," Martin said, giving him a baffled look. "It's not as good as Mrs. Radcliffe, but the author spins a pretty tale. In fact, what happens is, the hero and heroine are fleeing to Scotland together with the villain in hot pursuit, and they decide to take the long route, up the east coast, attempting to throw him off their tracks. It's what started me wondering if Troilus would head for Gretna or take the other route."

"Yes, you said that was something you'd read." Theo's eyes narrowed, focusing on the bookmark, very clearly in the first chapter. "Wait, wait. You're reading it for the *second time?*"

He asked that with an intensity that left Martin bewildered and slightly unnerved. "Yes, why should I not? The author repays it, I think. They aren't great works, but they're entertaining, and the villain is particularly amusing. And it seemed appropriate for our journey."

"Indeed." Theo sat back. "Maybe you could take some tips from the villain. How to catch a runaway heiress."

"He stabs the heroine in the back before she can make her vows, rather than see her marry the hero," Martin said. "I don't imagine the Conroys would be pleased if I did that. In any case, we're not the villains. We're the heroes, riding to the rescue."

"Us? We're the hero's loyal friends, at best. I'm probably the trickster servant. Or the clown."

Martin grinned. "What does that make me?"

"The noble companion who sacrifices himself for the heroine in the third volume," Theo said promptly. "You fling yourself in front of an assassin's knife for her sake. Watch out for that."

"Thank you, I shall. I should like to know why I couldn't be the hero, though."

"You're insufficiently virtuous," Theo said with a flicker of the eyelids, a tiny movement that had a wholly disproportionate effect on Martin's prick. "And excessively burdened with individuality. If you just stood around nobly, parroting trite phrases of love, I daresay you'd do very well."

"You have a point," Martin was forced to admit. "I enjoy Mrs. Radcliffe greatly, but her heroes are dreadful bores. And as for this author"—he indicated his novel—"hers are astonishingly bad. You'd think she'd never met a man. I'd certainly wager she's never been intimately acquainted with one."

Theo choked explosively on a mouthful of sausage, and Martin forgot about the literary conversation in the hurry to thump him on the back and find him a napkin.

"Have you enquired about our quarry here?" he asked, once Theo had recovered himself.

"Not yet. I felt coffee was more pressing. Oh, very well." Theo pushed away his plate and went to consult the landlord. Martin set himself to finishing his food, until he was startled by a loud exclamation in a deep voice. He looked up and saw the landlord striding over, with Theo and a serving maid at his heels.

"You're in search of a lady, for her parents, sir," the host said. "Is that right?"

"It is," Martin said. "Do you know something?"

"We had a pair of guests last night." Martin had to work to make out the landlord's meaning through his thick burr. "Lady and a gentleman. Dined in the private parlour."

"Describe the lady," Martin said, half rising. "Please."

"She was veiled when I saw her. But she asked for attendance."

"Didn't have a maid of her own," the girl put in. "Although she was travelling with a gentleman." She pursed her lips.

"Did you attend her? What was she like?"

"Very young. It's a pity and a shame," the girl added piously. "No more than eighteen, if that. Brown hair, dark, with a lovely curl to it, and one of them noses like a pug dog."

Miss Conroy's retroussé nose was considered one of her most appealing features. If she'd been poor, it would just have been called snub.

"And the gentleman?" Martin asked.

"Light hair. Not yaller, more your sort of colour, sir," the maid said, indicating Theo. "But the other was a handsome gentleman."

"Handsome is as handsome does," the innkeeper said firmly. "It was an elopement, then? It looked that way, I'll admit."

"Did she seem well?" Martin asked. "Distressed?"

"I'd say . . . if I may speak frankly? I'd say the young lady was in a towering bad temper. The gentleman was very attentive to her, but he fair bit my head off when she'd retired."

"About that," Theo said. "Did they take one room or two?"

Martin set his teeth, but it had to be asked, and he was grateful for it when the landlord replied. "Two, sir, and Liza had a truckle bed in with the lady. The gentleman didn't pay for that, but it seemed to me we ought to make sure."

"Thank you." Martin had rarely felt more grateful. "Thank you so much. Let me meet his obligation."

"No need for that, sir. We're decent folk here, and it was what was right."

"Then would you take something to set by for the next young lady in distress?" Martin suggested. The landlord agreed to that compromise. Martin added ten shillings for Liza, to fix her act of chaperonage in her memory should it be needed, made a note of the inn's name and direction, and hurried outside.

"They left at seven this morning," Theo said as the chaise moved off. He'd given the postilion orders to make all the haste they could. "Curse it. I should have asked when we arrived."

"So they're just two hours ahead of us now. They must have met with some accident yesterday. We could catch them before tonight if we're lucky."

"We'll need to stop at every inn we pass come evening," Theo pointed out.

"Were they able to describe the coach?"

"Nothing of use. A plain-coloured chaise, they said. We don't want to overshoot them."

"No," Martin said. "Especially not if Miss Conroy is losing enthusiasm for the journey." He exhaled. "I will admit, that worries me. If she's changing her mind now, or coming to regret her choice . . ."

"That puts him in a nasty position," Theo said slowly. "It's one thing to elope, quite another to drag an unwilling woman to the altar. Unwilling and under age. Of course, she might have just felt as though she'd had enough of the journey last night. Lord knows I have."

"True enough." Martin grimaced. "On the one hand, I don't want Troilus finding himself in a desperate position. Desperate men do desperate deeds, and this journey will have cost him a pretty penny and put him in jeopardy of the law. On the other, I can't deny it will be easier if she's pleased to see me than if we have to, ah, enforce her return."

"You're hoping she'll fall into your arms, sobbing, 'My hero!'?" Theo raised a sardonic eyebrow. "You've forgotten your role. Noble doomed companion, remember?"

Martin gave him a reproving look. "You read too many romances."

"Who says I read romances?"

"You obviously do, you know them well enough. The improving works of Dorothea Swann—" He stopped dead.

"I don't have to—" Theo began hastily.

"Dorothea Swann," Martin repeated. "*Dorothea Swann?* Theodore, Dorothea?"

"Look, I daresay you think you're very clever—"

"It's you, isn't it? That's why you recognised the book by its binding. And you said you were a scribbler." Martin found he was sitting upright. Theo, by contrast, was hunched into the corner of the carriage, hiding his face. "You're Dorothea Swann. You *are.*"

"It pays well," Theo said into his hands. "That's all."

"It is not all. They're marvellous."

Theo uncurled with speed. "You said they weren't as good as Mrs. Radcliffe."

"I did not. Well, maybe I did, but everyone can't be Mrs. Radcliffe. I've read all of Mrs. Swann. Of you."

"You said I can't write heroes," Theo said doggedly. Martin had never met a writer before, but he had heard it remarked that, as a breed, their capacity to remember unkind reviews was extraordinary. "Astonishingly bad, is what you said."

"Well, they are, a bit," Martin was forced to admit. "But your villains are wonderful."

Theo's grey eyes lit, sun breaking through rain clouds. "*And,* Mr. St. Vincent, you suggested that the author of *Melusina* had clearly never known a man's touch. Which, under the circumstances—"

"I resign all claim to literary criticism."

"Good. You're obviously unqualified."

"And you're extremely talented." Martin reached out, took his hand. "I mean it, Theo. I'm astounded. I'm proud to know you."

Theo looked at him, down at the hand that gripped his, up to Martin's face. Then he slid off the seat and manoeuvred himself around.

"What are you doing?" Martin demanded, although it was quite evident what he was doing. "Theo, for God's sake!"

Theo nudged his legs apart and settled between them, hands sliding up Martin's thighs. "Enlivening the journey?"

"On this road?" Martin demanded, as the chaise bumped. "If we go over a pothole you'll bite it off!"

"Give me a little credit." Theo pushed both thumbs up together, stroking them firmly over the tight cloth that confined Martin's balls. Martin gasped, and found he was spreading his legs wider. Theo gave a little satisfied purr, repeating the rolling movement until Martin couldn't have counselled discretion for a hundred pounds. And after all, the postilion wouldn't see, or hear, riding outside as he was. There was probably no place safer in England than a moving coach. He let his head drop back as Theo's hands went to the buttons of his breeches, unfastening the front fall, delving past his drawers.

"Tomcat," he whispered.

"Meow," Theo said, and ran his tongue over the head of Martin's prick.

"Oh Lord." Martin gripped the strap with one hand, got the other into Theo's hair, let himself luxuriate in the feeling of mouth and tongue. No teeth: Theo was covering them with his lips. The coach lurched again, and Theo made a muffled noise that might have been a curse, but he didn't stop his gamahuching, lavishing Martin's stand with pleasure. He was breathing hard through his nose, the sound mingling with Martin's harsh gasps.

He pulled away, just a little. "Christ, I love your prick. Talk to me. Tell me how you want it while I suck you."

Martin looked down, startled, and realised Theo was fumbling at his own buttons.

"Uh—like this." Theo shot a glare up, since his mouth was again occupied. Martin gathered his scattering wits. "With you on your knees. Seeing how hard you get with a prick in your mouth. Are you hard?" Theo moaned assent. "Is that from serving me? Take it deeper. God, yes, like that. And frig yourself harder. I want you to spend with me in your mouth."

Theo's noises suggested that was very possible. His hand was moving fast, and he was sucking Martin frantically, mouth so hot and wet and tight.

"I am going to fuck you tonight, on your knees, just as you are now," Martin told him. "You lovely wanton—oh *Christ*." He lurched forward, doubling over with the force of his climax, spending so hard that his bollocks spasmed painfully, and only realised as his pleasure ebbed that he'd more or less rammed himself down Theo's throat to do it.

He released his grip on the fine brown hair—he'd held it tight enough that his fingers had cramped—and looked down at the kneeling man with a surge of guilt. "Are you all right?"

"That depends." Theo sounded hoarse and breathless, not angry. "Do you think whoever owns this chaise wanted the upholstery soaked in milt? Because it's ankle-deep down here right now."

Martin started laughing. He was still shaking as he pulled Theo off his knees and up to kiss him openmouthed, and held him, half-dressed and panting as the chaise rattled on to the north.

They made excellent time to Boroughbridge, where they had to decide whether to go west for Gretna or stay on the Great North Road. The horses had been fresh at each stage and the road surface not dreadful, and they'd arrived in the little town before three o'clock.

It was quite extraordinarily busy. There was a horse fair on, along the very stretch of the Great North Road that ran through the town, with drovers and traders and farmers roaming the wide street and the scent of hay, sweat, and manure strong in the air. There were also a lot of inns, and Martin's heart sank. How would they find any individual in this bustle? The Crown Inn opposite had a front the width of four houses and claimed it could accommodate over a hundred guests, and there were several other coaching inns in view.

"We need to ask around," Theo said. He'd restored himself to as much neatness as ever he achieved, and looked quite respectable, but Martin couldn't stop seeing him as he had been, red-lipped, gasping, flushed with arousal. It seemed as though everyone around them must surely see their criminal conversation, as if it were written on both their faces. "That's assuming they changed horses here, of course. If not, we'll have to hope somebody saw them and noticed which way they went."

"We'll split up to ask." At least that way nobody would see him with Theo, nobody would guess.

Theo grimaced. "Would you leave it to me?"

"It'll take hours," Martin objected.

"Not really. I'm used to asking the right questions by now, and the town's not so large as all that. You wait for me, have something to eat."

Martin felt a little guilty at how much he wanted to accept that, and a little feeble too. It was only asking questions. But he was so damned tired of being gawped at, and Theo's care was as warming as the feel of his mouth. "Well—"

"Let me," Theo said. "Please."

Martin gave in to the indulgence. "Very well. If you don't mind."

Theo's smile looked just a little tense. "I shouldn't offer if I did."

Martin wished he could touch him, just a hand to the arm. He could; surely nobody would think twice, but he knew he would feel unbearably conspicuous. "Thank you, Theo," he said, low. "I cannot tell you how glad I am you're with me."

Colour surged up into Theo's cheeks. For just a second his expression was so raw that Martin wanted to demand what was wrong, then he gave his sly smile. "I hope you'll be saying that this evening. Come to that, I hope I will be."

They arranged to meet at the Black Bull inn, at the far end of the high street, slightly less busy than the inns on the Great North Road itself, and Theo set off.

Martin regretted the decision almost at once. It was easier to ignore the stares when he was with a companion. Now he felt not just alone but isolated. And under that, something else, he realised. He was lonely.

That wasn't a familiar sensation. Martin liked to be master of his own space, and time, and acquaintance. Solitude was a comfort to him, a proof of his independence, not a thing to fear. But he'd had Theo with him almost every moment of the last day and a half, and he realised with some surprise, he'd not wished the fellow away for any of that. He'd liked being with him, talking when there was something to say, sitting in silence without discomfort. He was going to miss him when this was over.

He made a good meal at the Black Bull without incident—there were simply too many people here to make him noteworthy; he should have been more determined and rejected Theo's offer, he told himself—and found a bench on which to sit outside the ancient inn to enjoy *Melusina* in the June sunshine, despite the to and fro of people. Theo approached not long after, munching on a slab of sticky dark-brown cake.

"What on earth are you eating?"

Theo offered it to him. Martin took a cautious bite and tasted ginger. "Apparently it's called parkin," Theo said. "I take no responsibility whatsoever."

"Of course you don't." Martin licked the crumbs from his lips and saw the way Theo's eyes followed his tongue. "Any luck?"

"Yes. Yes, I . . . Martin?"

"Mmm?"

Theo hesitated, then said in a rush, "What if Miss Conroy wants to go with him? What if she wants to marry him? You said we'd enforce her return. Did you mean it?"

Curse his doglike way with a question. Martin stared out, along the street, at the brand-new brick houses that showed the town's prosperity and the lower, crooked, whitewashed fronts of buildings from earlier years. "I don't know. Surely, whatever she may think, this way of going about things is not for the best."

Theo sat heavily on the bench next to him. "And who is to decide that for her? You? Is it your responsibility?"

"Her parents have the right, and they gave me the authority—"

"To bring her back. That's not authority, that's doing their bidding."

"Do you believe this man means well by her?" Martin asked. "Really? That he will be a good husband, that he will think of her as much as of her money, that this is the start to a happy marriage?"

"Probably not." Theo looked hunted. "But it could be."

"Is this your romantic streak?"

"Don't joke. I want to know, Martin. I know how much it means to you that you bring her back well and—and unmarried. Oh, hellfire. You have to bring her back, whatever she wants, don't you?"

Martin took a deep breath. "No."

"What?"

"I don't have to do what the Conroys want. If I bring her back against her will to settle my business with them—"

"You owe them nothing." Theo's voice was savage. "Nothing."

"It doesn't matter," Martin said. "I will not choose my course on the grounds that it's what they want me to do. If I did that, I'd still be wearing their collar." Theo shuddered. "We will catch up with Miss Conroy, and we will ask what she wants. And if it seems right to let her go her way, then we will do so, and she and her husband will have to take the consequences of their acts in due course." The certainty rolled through him as he spoke. "My responsibility here is any man or woman's responsibility: to stop a wrong being done. If I don't see a wrong to Miss Conroy, I shan't intervene."

It would, of course, deeply wrong her father if his daughter married without his consent, since Miss Jennifer was Mr. Conroy's to give away in law. That, Martin decided, was Mr. Conroy's bad luck. If he'd wanted someone to do his bidding without thought or question, he shouldn't have sent a free man.

Not that he had any faith at all in Troilus's good intentions. But even so, this felt like a knot unpicked in the mesh of conflicting wants and needs around him, and he'd unpicked it because of Theo's interest. Because he was no longer alone with his thoughts.

Martin wanted to reach out, grasp Theo's hands, but when he caught his travelling companion's eye, Theo simply gave a weak smile and shook his head.

"What's wrong?" Martin asked. "You look—"

"Exhausted," Theo interrupted. "My arse simply isn't up to this." He tipped his head back and inhaled deeply. "I found the inn they stopped at. Our runaways have stayed on the Great North Road and they're heading up the east coast. Not to Gretna."

"Dear heaven." Martin could have kissed him: for finding that out; for his insignificant, unnoticeable face that let him ferret out the information they needed without anybody thinking twice; for being angry on his behalf when Martin had been alone with his anger for so long. "If you hadn't found that out—if you hadn't written the book in the first place, come to that—I should have charged up to Gretna and not stood a chance. Thank you."

"Thank me when you return the young lady to her parents' eternal gratitude," Theo said. "Let's go and catch them up."

CHAPTER SIX

They spotted the coach at about eight o'clock that evening.

It had been a long journey from Boroughbridge. Theo had been silent and withdrawn for an hour or more. He seemed tired, perhaps unwell. Concerned, even, for Martin and the decisions he might have to make? Certainly he looked almost sick with worry, and Martin didn't know why. It wasn't, after all, Theo's affair; he would lose nothing if they failed, or chose not to succeed.

It had flitted through Martin's mind that he'd never said Theo would be paid whatever the outcome, and it felt too late to say it now, as though that would degrade the partnership they'd formed. Theo wasn't doing this for the money anymore, even though he needed it, Martin was sure. Theo cared.

Martin wasn't quite sure why Theo cared, nor why his caring meant so much. But he did, and it did. Inexplicably, unexpectedly, Martin had found a friend on this journey, and the thought warmed him in the cooling evening air. A friend who listened and understood, who stood by him, and of course it helped that he fucked like a wild animal.

Martin only wished he knew what was wrong.

The last few stages had been dismally frustrating, since they'd had to stop at every coaching inn they passed for fear they might overshoot their quarry. They'd agreed they'd keep going while the light lasted, which seemed to be hours longer than in London, and the sun was still bright and hot when their chaise had pulled in at the Farmers Arms, a yellow-grey brick building in Brompton on Swale.

There was only one chaise in the yard. It was painted bright blue with red shafts and wheels, but coated with the dust of long travel.

"That can't be it," Martin said. "We're looking for something unobtrusive. Everyone would have remembered that."

"They would, wouldn't they?" Theo stared at it. "You don't want to look in here?"

"No, of course we must. It will mean we can get out of this blasted chaise anyway."

Inside, the inn had a few customers. All men, of course; all white. Martin went to the woman behind the bar, since Theo was hanging back. "The coach outside, madam. Who came in it?"

She swept him with a long, assessing look. "Who's asking?"

"I'm seeking a young lady, travelling with a gentleman. A very young lady, with dark brown hair. I'm a friend of her family."

"A friend to the lady."

"To her family," Martin repeated. "I have a very urgent message from her parents to deliver. Do you have a pair of travellers of that description here?"

"Well, I do," the landlady said. "Whether it's the folk you want, I couldn't say. They've taken the private parlour. Lucy, show the gentleman to the parlour, will you?"

A serving maid approached, eyes widening as she took Martin in, but she bobbed a curtsey without comment.

He glanced around. Theo was behind him, lips pressed together. "It may be them. Will you come?"

"It's probably better if I don't," Theo said. "Discretion. You know. The lady's feelings."

"Theo, what's wrong?"

"Just go and get her. I'll wait." He turned away.

Martin wanted to take him by the shoulder, but he had Miss Jennifer to think about, and if this was not the pair he sought, a long way yet to go. "Very well, sit down. Have a drink. I'll be back soon."

Lucy led him down a narrow, low corridor to a door, and knocked. A male voice called, "Come in."

She poked her head round the door. "Beg your pardon for the trouble, sir, madam, but there's a gentleman." She bobbed again and retreated hastily.

Martin pushed the door wide. There were two people in the parlour, looking round at him. He had just a brief impression of a well-dressed man rising from his seat, because all his attention was fixed on the young lady whose teacup slipped from her fingers and fell to the floor.

"*Martin?*" said Jennifer Conroy.

"Miss Jennifer." Martin's legs were suddenly weak with relief. He came in, shutting the door. "Are you all right?"

"Who the devil are you, sir?" demanded the man. Troilus, Martin had to assume. "I did not invite you in."

"Your parents asked me to come after you, since your father could not come himself," Martin said, ignoring Troilus. "They are very worried for you. Will you come home?"

Miss Jennifer's mouth trembled. She shot a glance at her swain, looked back at Martin. "I can't. I'm . . . I'm going to get married."

"You can come home," Martin repeated. "I will take you. Nobody can stop you."

"But I have to get married," Miss Conroy whispered. "Geoffrey said . . ."

Troilus, who was rather red in the face, wasn't the dashing rake of Martin's vague imaginings. Medium height, with light-brown hair, a slim build padded out by his tailor. Not a repulsive specimen by any means; in fact, he looked not unlike Theo might, given money for a decent set of clothes and a good barber. But he was no Adonis, and he was also at least ten years too old to blame this kind of roguery on youthful enthusiasm.

"I am a friend of the lady's parents, sir. Kindly let me speak to her in private."

"Leave my betrothed in a room alone with a strange man? Certainly not."

"Oh, Geoffrey, this is *Martin*," Miss Jennifer said. "Martin St. Vincent, Geoffrey Hazelwood. Martin lived with us for years."

"Does the gentleman have your permission to leave us?" Martin pressed.

"Whatever you have to say can be said in front of me," Hazelwood said. "Miss Conroy is my affianced bride."

"She is not. She is seventeen years old, and you do not have her parents' consent," Martin retorted, and realised too late that was a mistake as Miss Jennifer's face set into a familiar pout.

"You see, Jennifer?" Hazelwood appealed to her. "This man is come to make you do your parents' bidding, without the slightest regard for the wishes of your heart. He's here to separate us. Well, we will not be separated." He reached out his hand, and Miss Jennifer took it.

God give me strength. "Miss Jennifer," Martin said. "If you truly, earnestly wish to marry Mr. Hazelwood, you know very well your father will not stand in your way."

"He will! He wants me to marry a lord!"

"Yes, he does, but more than that, he wants your happiness. You can twist him round your little finger, you know that. If he believes that this is the right marriage for you, then he will see you wed to Mr. Hazelwood—"

"But Mother—"

"With enough ceremony to delight Mrs. Conroy's heart," Martin went on over her. "Come, Miss Jennifer. They aren't cruelly bent on sacrificing you on the altar of worldly advancement. Of course they should like to see you well up in the world, but do you really think they would deny you your heart's wish if this is a lasting attachment? When have you ever been denied what you wanted?"

"You were not permitted to correspond with me," Mr. Hazelwood put in.

The arsehole. "Sir, you did not bring your suit to the lady's father as a gentleman should," Martin said. "If you pay court in the proper manner, if Miss Conroy's attachment is lasting—"

"And wait for years to have their permission?" Hazelwood struck in.

"Why?" Martin asked. "Aren't you prepared to wait for her?"

"Stop it!" Miss Jennifer flung a hand up. "Stop talking about me. *I* am not prepared to wait for years, or have Mother and Father decide for me."

"There is no need to talk of years." Martin had a worrying sense that he was losing this argument. "Or even months. But why this rush to Scotland, when you could be married in the eyes of the world?

Why deny yourself all the preparations for a wedding and the pleasures of it, and your parents the chance to see their only child wed? You may not wish to marry into Society, but surely you wish to be received. And a border marriage—"

Miss Jennifer's face crumpled. Martin pressed his advantage. "You will only marry once, Miss Jennifer. One wedding, one chance, one day. Why must it be this way? Why is this gentleman in such a hurry?"

"Don't listen, Jennifer," Hazelwood said. "You and I know the truth. My love . . ." He dropped to one knee. "You know I should have preferred to court you in the proper fashion. You know this was forced on us. You know I have promised that you will never regret confiding me your heart and hand."

I know when quarter day is, Martin wanted to say, but he was sufficiently familiar with Miss Jennifer's response to contradiction; he must not drive her into this fellow's arms by questioning her judgement. "Sir," he said instead. "I want only to know that Miss Jennifer is well, happy, and safe. If you want that, then you and I have the same goal."

Hazelwood shot him a glare of intense dislike. "Handsomely said, sir."

"I have no right to take you anywhere against your will," Martin added to Miss Jennifer, "and you know I should not try. You have kicked me in the shins quite often enough."

She gave a gurgle of laughter and clapped a hand to her mouth. "Oh, I was a terribly naughty child."

"And yet, I still wish you well," he assured her. "Somehow. Please, may I speak to you, alone? To put my mind at rest?" She looked just a little uncertain. "You cannot imagine I should try to persuade you when your mind is made up. I know you a little too well for that."

Miss Jennifer hesitated, eyes darting between the two men. Martin thought she seemed undecided, and that gave him a flare of hope. "I can't enforce you," he went on. "I only want to be sure of your heart."

"Really, Geoffrey," Miss Jennifer said. "There is no reason why not. I have known Martin all my life. And after all, we will have to—to justify our decision when we are married. Please excuse us."

Hazelwood hesitated, clearly weighing up his options. "As you wish, my dear. But remember, there will be those who try to separate us. I will keep faith with you, my love. Keep it with me."

He stooped to press a passionate kiss to her fingers, exchanged a blank look with Martin, and left the room. Martin knew a strong wish that Theo was with him, just to exchange a roll of the eyes. He would relish his pithy opinion of this cheapjack fraud.

He sat opposite Miss Jennifer. She offered him a smile that wasn't quite as confident as she probably meant it to be.

"Miss Jenny," he said gently. "You know I want your happiness. Will this really make you happy? A runaway wedding, whispers, backs turned, your parents' distress? The gentleman feels such affection for you; surely he will be willing to wait a little longer rather than inflict disgrace on your good name?"

She twined her fingers together. "But I don't want to wait." It didn't sound happy, or impatient. "I *can't*. It's too late now."

"Of course it's not. You can come home and nobody will know. Mr. Hazelwood won't speak of this, will he? And who else is there?" Except Theo, of course. Martin made a mental note to keep him out of the way if possible. "You haven't ruined yourself, you are not compromised. This was an indiscretion, but it does not have to shape the course of your life. I don't ask you to reconsider your affections, Miss Jenny. Just to give yourself more time."

She bit her lip. "I don't think I can. And I promised Geoffrey."

"A gentleman will not hold you to that promise."

"It seemed like such a wonderful game." Her voice held the threat of tears. "I thought eloping would be an adventure, and it was, but— I wish I'd done it differently. I keep thinking of what Papa will say."

"He will welcome you home with open arms," Martin said. "And if you are escorted back by Mr. Hazelwood, if Mr. Hazelwood shows that he puts your happiness and well-being before his own satisfaction, I imagine your father will very soon be persuaded of his true worth." He was absolutely sure that Mr. Conroy would have a very good idea of Hazelwood's worth, no matter what wheedles the fellow cut; he was equally sure that nothing would persuade Hazelwood to renounce the chance of an immediate marriage when he was so close to his goal. If he could only persuade Miss Jennifer to ask for more time, he was quite sure the man would show his true colours.

Her hands tightened. "Do you think—"

"You little bastard!"

Martin and Miss Jennifer both jumped in shock. The bellow had been one of unrestrained fury, it had come from the direction of the taproom, and it was Hazelwood's voice. "Swine!" He was shouting now. "Treacherous damned swine!"

"That's Geoffrey!" Miss Jennifer said, eyes wide. "What on earth—"

"I'll find out." Martin ran into the corridor and through, and saw the tableau. The few customers gawping, the outraged landlady with hands on hips, Hazelwood and Theo standing face-to-face in the middle of the taproom. Hazelwood's hand was curled into a fist as though he would strike.

Martin skirted round them. Hazelwood's face was red with anger and what seemed to be real indignation. Theo looked . . .

Caught. He looked as though he'd been caught.

"You worthless hound," Hazelwood was saying. "You damned liar. And after all we did for you. I had your promise, curse you. You had my money!"

"What?" Martin couldn't take this in: Hazelwood's outrage; the wretched guilt on Theo's face.

"Well, you'll pay for it, you little cheat," Hazelwood said viciously, ignoring him. "I'll have every penny you owe me or I'll see you gaoled for it." He swung round, jabbing a finger at Martin. "I daresay you think you're clever, suborning him, but he'll sell your skin as fast as he sold mine, as soon as there's a higher bidder in the offing. Won't you, *cousin*?"

Theo twitched. Martin stared at him.

"And as for coming here pretending you'd give me a fair hearing," Hazelwood added to Martin, a little louder. "Cozening Miss Conroy with promises of listening to her, pretending you did not know me, when all the time you had my wheedling, deceitful cousin accompanying you? For shame, sir. It is hardly fair to misrepresent yourself so."

Martin didn't have to look round to know Miss Jennifer was there; the triumphant look in Hazelwood's eyes was enough. "I am as surprised as you," he said, attempting to keep his voice even. "I was under the impression that Mr. Swann was helping me in my search. That he was as ignorant as I as to who you were. It seems we have both been played for fools."

Theo's mouth moved. He didn't speak.

"I'll talk to you later," Martin said, to Theo's shoulder. He couldn't quite make himself look at the man's face. "Miss Jennifer, can we finish our conversation?"

"I think you have shown your hand, sir," Hazelwood said, very nearly suppressing the triumph in his voice, and went to Miss Jennifer. "I am sorry, my dear, that any friend of yours should act so duplicitously. But that man there is my cousin, who demanded, nay, *extorted* money from me not to betray our destination, and you must judge Mr. . . . ." He flapped a dismissive hand at Martin. "His claims for yourself."

"I had no idea," Martin repeated. "Miss Jennifer—"

She shook her head, lips clamped together. Hazelwood took her arm. "Come," he said gently and steered her back to the private parlour.

Martin couldn't move for a second, stunned by defeat, and then turned back to look at Theo. "Cousin."

"I. Uh."

That seemed to be all he had. They stood in silence that grew and twisted between them, tangled itself around Martin's throat, stole all the air from the room.

"May I speak?" Theo asked at last.

Martin grabbed his arm and dragged him out to the inn yard, careless of the fascinated audience, pulling him as far as possible from the building before the words could no longer be contained. "What the devil? What the *hell*?"

Theo swallowed hard. "Well, it's true. That's all. It's true."

"But what's true? What did he mean, 'cousin'? You took his money? For what?" Martin demanded, but he already knew. "You've known who he was, who Troilus was, all along. Haven't you?"

"Not at first," Theo insisted, as though it mattered. "Not when you first asked. Only after the last advertisement."

"But..." Martin didn't even know what to say. "I don't understand. Why did you do this? Why did you help me if—" His voice cracked.

Theo flinched. "When this started, I hadn't any more idea who Troilus was than the man in the moon. I didn't know his handwriting, or care either. I was helping you, truly. I meant to. But when I went to the White Horse Cellar . . . I told you nobody there could identify him. I told you he'd already gone." He shut his eyes. "I lied."

Martin took that in. "She was still there? You could have stopped her setting off, ruining herself? You could have prevented all of this and instead—what? *Why*?"

"Because she was with my cousin," Theo said dully. "Geoffrey."

"I find it *very* hard to believe you're related to a gentleman."

Theo did not react to the contempt in his voice. "My mother married beneath her. A poor curate. I saw Geoffrey there, I asked his intentions, and he told me he intended to take her off to Gretna."

"And what did you ask for to keep that nugget of information to yourself?"

"He offered," Theo said thickly. "I owe him money. He offered to forgive my debt, and I accepted, and I—" He cleared his throat. "I advised him to go up the Great North Road. To evade pursuit. He was pleased with that."

"You pretended you didn't know about the different routes to the border," Martin said. "I only thought of that because of the book you had written, but you pretended not to know. Would you have mentioned they might not go to Gretna, if I hadn't said so? Why did you agree to come with me at all?" He could hear his voice rising, couldn't quite control it.

"You offered me forty pounds."

"You asked me for that!"

"Well, I didn't think you'd agree! How should I have turned that down?"

"So you came with me—what, intending to mislead me? Planning to let me go up to Gretna on a wild-goose chase, while that rogue forced Miss Conroy into marriage?"

"Yes. That's exactly what I meant to do." Theo met his eyes for the first time. "Does it count at all that I didn't?"

"You've been lying to me from the start." Martin's breath was coming short, his throat tight. "Every word. And last night? What was that for?"

"If I said, because I like you, would you believe me?"

"*Believe* you?"

"I could have told you they'd gone to Gretna Green at Boroughbridge," Theo said. "Or just let you decide which way to go for yourself. You'd have picked Gretna. Geoffrey would have secured his rich marriage and written off my debt, *and* you'd have paid me forty pounds. And you'd have thought it was just bad luck, and you wouldn't hate me now."

"Are you asking me to be grateful you didn't betray me?" Martin's fists were clenched so hard they hurt. "Am I supposed to *thank* you for that? You've been making a mockery of me for days, and you'd like me to be happy that you stopped?"

"It wasn't a mockery!" Theo hissed. "For God's sake! Why should I have cared? Why should Miss Conroy have grown men chasing over the country to save her from her stupidity? I've worked every bloody hour in the day for seven years to keep myself afloat with a damned great millstone around my neck, and when I saw a chance to free myself, I took it. Wouldn't you have?"

"Not at that price."

Theo set his teeth. "Is there any chance at all that I could explain and you would listen?"

"I have listened," Martin said. "I listened to you. You listened to me." They had talked—*he* had talked so intimately. Theo had known what success meant to him almost better than he had himself. And still he had deceived Martin, lied to him by word and omission, all the way through, from that first claimed ignorance.

"You lied about the chaise," he said slowly. "You didn't tell me what it looked like. Did you really ask as we went about where they had gone, or was that invented? I suppose there was no need to make the effort, since you had no intention of finding them. How far ahead they were, where they were going, it was all a lot of nothing, wasn't it? And then—last night."

"Martin—"

"You said, because you like me, but still you didn't stop lying to me. Even then, even after last night, you didn't decide whose side you were on." It hurt extraordinarily. "You didn't decide until this afternoon, not until Boroughbridge, did you? You were still ready to let him carry her off, and thanks to you he will doubtless do that now."

"And not forgive my debt either," Theo said through his teeth. "I know. I'm sorry. I'm sorry I failed and I'm sorry I'm not a better man and—I'm sorry."

"So am I," Martin said. "I trusted you and you made me a fool."

"If you would listen—"

"Can you tell me that Miss Conroy will not marry your cousin?" Martin asked. "Because if you can't tell me that, you have nothing to say that I want to hear." He took out his purse and extracted a couple of guineas. His hands were shaking a little. "Here. Find your own way back to London. I don't want to see you again."

CHAPTER SEVEN

After that, it was inevitable that they had to share a bedchamber. "I've no more space," the landlady said, fixing Theo with a glare. "We're not a big house, and I've Mr. Hazelwood and the young lady to accommodate."

"How far is the next inn?"

"No more than eight miles."

It was a sign of how deeply miserable Theo was that he considered that for several minutes. He could walk away from the lot of them. Let the petulant, pampered Miss Conroy make her mistakes; let Geoffrey claim his fortune attached to a bride, and doubtless send Theo to a debtor's prison in vengeance for his useless treachery. Let Martin stay here, unhappy and alone and defeated, because Theo was contemptible.

He should have walked to the next inn, or slept in a hedgerow if he had to, but instead he had two glasses of gin, sitting alone and staring into the calamity of every decision he had ever made, and after that he simply couldn't find the strength.

If he wasn't a wretched, dishonest, treacherous, greedy liar, he would be sitting here with Martin now. They'd be talking, congratulating each other on having found the runaways and persuaded Miss Conroy to think twice. He'd be seeing the lines around Martin's eyes relax a little. He'd make him laugh.

And then they'd go upstairs, in an unobtrusive way, and lock the door, and Theo would drop to his knees and use his mouth until Martin couldn't wait another minute. Until he was bent over the bed, with Martin's hands hard on his hips and breath hot in his ear, giving each other the fuck they'd both wanted so much, and afterwards collapsing, limbs tangled, together.

He'd even bought oil in Boroughbridge as he wandered around, ducking into coaching inns for the look of the thing—which was to say, in order to keep up the lie he'd been telling Martin all along. What a waste of money. What a hopeless, stupid waste.

He dragged his travelling bag into the bedchamber and shut the door. Martin was sitting on the side of one bed, face in hands. He didn't look up. Theo hesitated, then sat on the other and took off his shoes. He moved in silence, but every creak of the floorboards and rustle of cloth was as loud as a shout.

"Out of interest," Martin said eventually. "How much?"

"How much for what?"

"How much was it that you sold me for?"

It was like a blow. Theo couldn't even make his mouth form the words he wanted to cry aloud. *I didn't! I changed my mind! I told you, in the end . . .*

Too little, too late.

"Does it matter?" he asked dully. "What difference would it make?"

"None at all. Miss Conroy has lost her trust in me, and is like to head off into this blighted marriage, and it's my fault for trusting you as I did, or for not paying you enough. I merely wondered what the price of your loyalty was. And whether you counted your body as part of that."

Theo's stomach contracted so hard that he feared he might vomit. "I told you. That wasn't—"

"It was because you liked me," Martin agreed. "God preserve me from your hatred, if this is how you treat those you like."

Theo rolled back onto the bed and lay, staring up at the rafters. "Seven hundred pounds down and seventy a year forever."

There was a short silence, then Martin said, incredulously, "*How* much?"

"I owe my cousin Geoffrey seven hundred pounds, and pay ten per cent interest on that sum yearly, no matter by how much I may reduce the principal. I have been paying for seven years. It has been the one motivating force of my life, to find a way to pay on time, because he and his father before him have always made the consequences of defaulting very clear."

He heard the other bed creak as Martin moved, but didn't look round. "How did you come to owe such a sum?"

Theo grimaced at the ceiling. "I was always destined to be a curate like my father, you see. All my education was directed towards that, and nobody thought to ask my opinion. But I did not want the Church, not at all, and once at university I soon found I preferred the company of sparks and knowing men. I thought I belonged in such company, and also, I thought I could play cards." He gave a mirthless laugh. "Well, I soon learned I was wrong about that. By my second year I found myself owing seven hundred pounds, to men who made it clear that it was not merely a debt of honour."

Martin didn't speak, but he was at least listening. Theo went on, his mouth feeling hard and awkward on the words. "My parents had nothing to help me with. They had given me everything they could as it was, and my uncle Hazelwood was already paying, grudgingly, for my education. He was not pleased to be asked for more, had a great deal to say on the topic of his sister's imprudent marriage, to her and to me. But once I had been sent down for gambling and nonpayment of debts, and it was clear that I was likely to have my legs broken for it, and my mother had begged him, weeping on her knees, then he lent me the money. With conditions, of course, to remind me of my abuse of his generosity. I must pay seventy pounds a year in interest, until every penny of the principal is repaid. Oh, and he can demand the whole outstanding sum at any time, and will prosecute me for debt if I default. That was a condition added to keep me in line, you understand."

"That's usury," Martin said.

"It may be, but I signed the agreement since I had no choice, and the Hazelwoods—first my uncle, now Geoffrey since the old bastard is dead, but he is not one whit kinder—have held that debt over my head ever since. I've paid nearly five hundred pounds in interest since then, and chiselled just ninety off the principal. I'll be paying it all my life." He smiled bitterly at the ceiling. "I agreed to their terms because I thought they'd be better than broken legs, but I have had cause to wonder about that since."

"Theo . . ."

"It killed my parents." He let the words stand, facing them in their starkness. "My father was furious with Uncle Hazelwood. My mother was caught between them. They were both so disappointed with me. Devastated. It aged them. I thought I might be able to mend matters, if I worked hard enough. But the typhus came before that day did." He breathed out, long and hard.

"And that's me. That's why I run the *Advertiser*, why I take every penny I can, why I write every moment I have. It's why I lied to you, and took your money under false pretences, and it's why I couldn't manage to tell you the truth until I was forced to make the choice at Boroughbridge. When I saw Geoffrey at the White Horse Cellar, I saw a chance to shed the burden on my back, and to be quite frank, I should have cheerfully let Miss Conroy marry him in order to be rid of my debt, if it had not been for you."

He heard Martin's sharp inhalation, but he would not conceal this. "You asked for the truth. Or perhaps you didn't, but you are getting it. And the truth is, I am tired of my life, I am tired of living under this weight, and I have no sympathy for Miss Conroy's stupidity."

"She's little more than a child."

"She's seventeen. I was nineteen when my uncle imposed the terms of my debt. And you were four when someone decided you'd make a thoughtful gift for a friend, so why the devil should Miss Conroy be immune to the cruelty of this shitty world?"

There was a long silence.

"But you told me the truth," Martin said at last. "At Boroughbridge, you told me where they were going. I would not have caught them up otherwise."

"For what good it has done. If I'd kept my mouth shut, one of us would have got something from this farce."

"And still, you didn't," Martin said. "You changed your mind. Why?"

Theo dropped his arm over his face, covering his eyes. "Ah, I don't know. Perhaps I am simply tired of the man I have become. I would rather be the man you thought I was."

"And will your cousin sue you for the debt now?"

"Certainly if this marriage doesn't come off. He probably will anyway. He holds grudges, and he has always resented anything his father gave me. It was all his by right, you see, and he does not like to give up anything that is his. Not to mention that he is in huge debt himself."

"How? Were they not well off?"

"Oh yes, a prospering landed family," Theo said with a shrug. "Uncle Hazelwood kept the lands up. But farming doesn't pay so much these days, what with the wars and the taxes, and certainly not when the landowner is in London playing at being a gentleman, rather than minding his affairs in the country. It's five years since my uncle died and Geoffrey has spent several times his income for every one of those. Clothes, horses, dice. He's mortgaged Felford Hall, but he won't sell it unless matters go beyond desperation. It allows him to cling to his gentlemanly pretensions, to be Hazelwood of Felford."

Martin frowned. "But will your seven hundred be enough to pay his debts?"

"Nothing like, even if I had seven hundred, which I do not. He'll send me to prison out of spite because I dared attempt to stop him claiming his fortune, which is to say Miss Conroy's money. That's his by right now, you see, in his mind."

"Theo." Martin said it meaningfully, and waited until Theo moved his arm and looked round. "Is your cousin as bad as you say? Truly?"

Theo sighed. "He is his own sun, the centre of his universe, and he does not forgive those who fail to give him due obeisance. If he marries Miss Conroy and her parents are insufficiently generous, he'll blame her for letting him down. The imprudence of the marriage will be all her fault. And if they are generous, he will take that as no more than his right, and very soon he'll be resenting her for any claim she makes on his money. Believe me, I know. I have given him close on six hundred pounds towards a seven-hundred-pound debt, and every time I come to pay him he behaves as though I've dipped my hand into his purse."

Martin's jaw was set. "I can't see her marry him. Not knowing this. But . . ."

Theo watched his face. "What?"

"Oh, the devil." Martin's hands tightened into fists. "I'm damned afraid that he's compromised her."

"In the sense of travelling without a chaperone?" Theo suggested, without much hope.

"In the sense of taking her to bed." Martin met his eyes. "You don't look surprised."

If Theo was, it was only that Martin should share his thoughts on this with him. But after all, nothing he could say would make it worse if those suspicions were true. "I don't know if I am. It's a contemptible thing to do, but what better way to secure the marriage?"

"And make her feel she has no choice now," Martin said grimly. "I think she wanted to listen to me, she believed I was on her side. But—"

"I ruined that," Theo said. "Played right into Geoffrey's hands, and undermined your standing with her. Ah, hell's tits. I'm sorry."

"I daresay you are, and it butters no parsnips," Martin said. "I don't want your apologies; I want to avert this calamity. I have been racking my brains up here for hours, and I simply cannot think what to do. Even if she has been imprudent, even if, God forfend, she's with child, there must be something I can do other than stand by and let her marry your greedy wretch of a cousin, but what? I intend to follow them to the border and be there in case she changes her mind up until the vows are spoken, but beyond that, I have no ideas at all." He stood, paced to the end of the room, and turned abruptly. "I can think of nothing other than carrying her off by force, and I'd be prepared to do that, except that I know damned well I should probably find myself gaoled for it and make matters a great deal worse. Curse it. What would happen if this was a Dorothea Swann book?"

"There would be a hero, of course. Someone to sweep Miss Conroy to safety and leave Geoffrey looking the fool he is. Some paper doll of a man with nothing to him, succeeding only because I shape the story to make it possible." Theo sat up, swinging his legs off the bed. "That's the problem, you see. When I write my books, I can make the world and its people do what I want. If I could do that in life, I should not have made such a damned mess of everything. Ah, the devil. If I were writing this story . . ."

Martin took another pace so that he was close by. Theo was painfully reminded of last night, when they had been like this: he was sitting on a bed, Martin standing before him. "What would you do?"

"Snatch Miss Conroy from under Geoffrey's nose. Watch you return her to her parents in triumph. Have you forgive me."

"Yes," Martin said, that deep voice so low it resonated in Theo's ears. "I should have preferred that story too. I thought that we worked well together, when I thought we worked together." He reached out to brush the hair off the side of Theo's face, very softly, as if soothing away a hurt that instead grew stronger with every touch. "I wish to God you had been who I believed you to be."

"So do I," Theo said, lips dry. "Very much."

"But you wanted to be free." Martin's fingers combed through Theo's hair, over his scalp, sending shudders down his spine. "I know. I would once have done a great deal for that too."

The blood rushed to Theo's face, burning, choking him with shame. "Don't. My God. I did this to myself, I know I did, and I have piled villainy on venality for years to escape the consequences of my own folly, and— I'm sorry, Martin. I'm sorry."

He couldn't find anything else to say, but Martin didn't seem to need anything. He stood, looking down, face grave, running his fingers through Theo's hair as if stroking a cat, and that gentle kindness was worse than anything he could have said.

Theo didn't want kindness. He'd rather have had rage at his betrayal, his stupid petty selfishness, than this dreadful acceptance, as though Martin had never really expected anything better. He wanted to make this right, he wanted to put himself back on his damned feet, at least until Geoffrey knocked him off them again, and he wanted Martin's hands touching him as they had before, not with this sense of mourning something lost.

That was not going to happen with his greed and guilt sitting between them like a toad. But what could he do? What weapon did he have that he could use against Geoffrey?

None. He didn't have anything. He was under Geoffrey's thumb, and they both knew it. If he was the hero in a tale, there would be some way to wriggle out from his obligations and make this right, but Theo well knew he was not a hero. He was so much better at villainy.

The thought flashed bright in his mind, like dry paper taking flame. He stared at Martin's waist, unseeing.

"Theo?"

"I think . . . Martin, listen. Will you listen to me?"

Martin's hand stopped its movement. "To what?"

Theo took a deep breath. "I have lied to you and let you down and caused this calamity, and there is no reason you should believe a word I say. With all that said, is there any chance you could trust me once more?"

"Trust you?" Martin's topaz eyes locked with his, steady and intent. His fingers still rested on Theo's cheek. Theo could feel the pulse of blood and wondered if it was a little faster than usual, or if that was his own. "To do what? For whose benefit?"

It wasn't cruelly said, but the words nevertheless made Theo flinch. "I know I've given you no reason to treat my intentions with anything but contempt. But if I said I wanted to help, that I wanted to do better, would you trust me? Could you do that?"

"No," Martin said, voice gentle and implacable as his eyes. "No, Theo. I don't think I could."

CHAPTER EIGHT

Theo knocked surreptitiously on the door of what he'd been told was Geoffrey's chamber near eleven o'clock that night. He waited a few moments, knocked surreptitiously again, and a little after that gave up and just banged loudly.

He was relieved to hear steps. He'd not been entirely sure Geoffrey wouldn't try to consolidate his position by slipping to his fiancée's bedroom once more. But here was his cousin, yawning in nightshirt and cap, opening the door with a scrape and a sleepy curse and recoiling in horror at the sight Theo presented.

"What the—"

"Let me in," Theo snarled, and pushed past him, clutching the scrap of raw beefsteak to his face.

"Good God, what happened to you? Did the black do that?" Geoffrey demanded. "It serves you right, you little turd."

"Be damned to you." Theo put the candlestick he carried on the mantelpiece next to the looking glass, removed the bloody meat, and peered at his rapidly swelling eye and lip.

"Looks painful," Geoffrey said with some satisfaction. "That will teach you to play both ends against the middle."

"It wasn't my fault," Theo snapped. "He paid me well to accompany him, and I never intended to catch you up. What, do you think I wanted to see your ugly face and throw away the chance of being relieved of your damned usury, you gouging miser?"

"Mind your tongue!"

"The devil I will." Theo swung to face him. "Do you think I shall show you respect as head of the family now? You've lost more money than ever I did, you pustulant prick, and if you're going to pursue me for debt, I see no reason to pretend I give a damn what you think anymore. Arsehole," he added, for good measure.

Geoffrey was openmouthed with startled fury. Theo turned back to the mirror, dabbing at his cut lip. It was extremely painful and swelling nastily already. "I expect you're wondering why I'm in here, apart from not wanting to share a room with that brute any longer—"

"You're not sharing this room! You can sleep in the stables like the dog you are."

"Very well," Theo said. "If you don't want to know what he's planning, I'll go. I don't give a curse if you secure your prize or end up swinging for rape or bleeding in a ditch; in fact, given the choice, I'd rather the latter."

"What?" Geoffrey demanded. "What was that?"

"I—hope—you—die—in—a—ditch," Theo said, as clearly as he could given his mouth felt afire. "To hell with you." He headed toward the door, picking up the candlestick.

Geoffrey seized his arm. "Wait. What did you mean by that? 'What he's planning'?"

"I thought you wanted me to sleep in the stables." Theo shook him off. "Listen, curse you. I've been dragged halfway across the country, thrashed, and insulted. I've lost out on my forty pounds that St. Vincent was to give me before you let him know I was a spy in his camp. If you want my help now, you'll bloody well pay for it."

Geoffrey wore the expression of a man who had just had a lapdog bite his fingers off. Theo had always been so careful to conciliate and appease him before, since he had been so hopelessly in his power. Now the worst had happened, and Theo found he was exulting in the wreckage.

"Well?" he demanded.

"Well—but—what?"

"I know what St. Vincent's orders are," Theo said. "And I know what he intends to do to bring the girl back to her home. And, on the subject, *he* knows that you've helped yourself to her maidenhead."

Geoffrey's cheeks flamed. "You won't speak like that of my fiancée."

"Oh, don't give me your flannel," Theo said contemptuously. "If you respected her, you wouldn't have tupped her."

Geoffrey didn't deny it. "What is it to you?"

"To me, nothing. To the Conroys' man, tasked by her father to bring her back in one piece?" He raised a brow. "What do you think?"

His cousin was no more a fighter than Theo was. He looked again at Theo's battered features with an expression of dawning alarm. "If that savage strikes me—"

"—and tells the local magistrate that you were running away with his master's daughter," Theo interrupted helpfully, "I'm sure that will go very well for you. I daresay magistrates *love* to aid bankrupts who are running away with underage heiresses."

"And you plan to help him, do you?" Geoffrey said bitterly. "Turning your back on your family?"

"My family, in your person, can go to the devil," Theo said. "And so can St. Vincent for what he has done to me, and so can Miss Conroy, the silly trollop. I'm for the highest bidder."

"If you want payment, you'll help me get Miss Conroy to the altar," Geoffrey retorted.

"You cancel my debt. The same bargain as before, but I'll have it in writing. You give me that, and I'll tell you what St. Vincent's got planned for you."

"No, you tell me what he has planned, and I'll see if it's worth my while to give you a penny."

"You've got this wrong," Theo said. "You think I'm still under your thumb, but I'm not. It's too late for that. You've hag-ridden me for years, and I'll be damned glad to see St. Vincent deal with you. Or I should, if he hadn't—" His hand crept up to his battered face. "I tell you this, Geoffrey: you won't like being on the receiving end of his temper or his fists. I thought he was going to murder me."

His cousin's appalled expression suggested he had no trouble believing that. It might have made Theo laugh if his eye and lip hadn't hurt so much. He pointed a finger at Geoffrey instead. "I'm damned tempted to let St. Vincent deal with you and see if you're in any state to pursue me for debt when he's finished with you—him, with the Conroys' wealth as a shield. But I should also like to serve the swine out myself for this insult. On the whole, I'd prefer to be secure just a fraction more than to see you get what you deserve, but it's a close-run thing. So." He planted his hands on his hips. "Take my terms or be damned to you."

Geoffrey hesitated. Theo snarled. "If you're not interested, I'm going to bed. To the settle downstairs," he added sourly. "Enjoy your night."

"Wait." Geoffrey visibly reached a decision. "For that price, you've to do more than just tell me his plans. I want your help getting the dog off my scent. And the bargain includes my marriage. If I can't get Miss Conroy to the altar, you get nothing."

Theo hesitated, glowering, but finally nodded grudging assent. "Very well. I want it in writing though. Is there a pen and ink?"

There was, the nib badly cut and the ink thick and lumpy. Theo considered, then wrote.

In consideration of Mr. THEODORE SWANN's assistance in aiding Mr. GEOFFREY HAZELWOOD to secure Miss CONROY's person in marriage, the said Mr. HAZELWOOD agrees to cancel Mr. SWANN's debt of Seven Hundred Pounds and all Interest on that sum forthwith, nor is any further sum to be due from Mr. SWANN on that debt, from the date of this Memorandum. This Agreement not to be affected by the Monies to come with Miss CONROY, whether she bring Riches or Nothing to Mr. HAZELWOOD's coffers.

"You can't put that," Geoffrey objected, looking over his shoulder.

"I can, and I damned well shall. I won't have you turn on me if your golden goose is barren of eggs. That's not my fault."

"If her father don't pay up, I shall be ruined," Geoffrey said. "I'll need the money from you then."

Theo found himself speechless. "I don't give a tinker's curse what you need," he managed at last. "I hope you starve. Are you expecting me to help you win a rich bride and then be your banker if you fail to get the funds? Go fry your face."

"I could be left with nothing," Geoffrey said obstinately. "Saddled with a worthless wife and still in debt."

"Or, you could have St. Vincent throw you into a ditch and not win her in the first place."

Geoffrey's face set in a mulish expression. "Half."

"What?"

"If I marry but the old man doesn't pay, I'll halve your debt. Three hundred and fifty, with interest of thirty-five a year."

Theo threw down the pen and pushed his chair back. "You are the greediest man alive."

"You're the one claiming my money," Geoffrey retorted. "Asking me to buy a pig in a poke for seven hundred pounds, when I might see no return on it? I am not such a fool. I'll take my chances with the other."

"I wish you joy," Theo said viciously. "I hope he beats you to a pulp. Very well, let us say, halve the debt if you marry and Conroy does not come up to scratch, but you will pay me two hundred if he does."

Geoffrey objected vociferously and a nasty but brief argument ended with Theo resentfully agreeing to the previous offer. His cousin, triumphant, scooped up the pen himself to write, striking out the disputed sentence and replacing it.

This Agreement to be affected by the Monies to come with Miss CONROY as follows: if she brings less than Five Hundred a Year to Mr. HAZELWOOD after the marriage, the Debt and Interest to be Halv'd. If more than Five Hundred, the Debt to be Cancell'd.

"Five hundred my arse," Theo said, once Geoffrey had finished writing. "Two."

They argued about that. Theo fixed immovably on three hundred, and Geoffrey grudgingly struck out the number and replaced it. He read the document over, and bent to write again:

If the Lady is not Secur'd to be Mr. HAZELWOOD's wife, the aforesaid Mr. SWANN has no claim on Mr. HAZELWOOD and his debt remains to be Paid in Full.

He sprinkled sand on the paper to blot the ink. Theo took the paper up, reading it over carefully.

"What now?" Geoffrey demanded.

"Just making sure. I do not intend to have you cheat me as your damned father did."

"He did not!"

"The terms he forced me to were usury," Theo said savagely. "I have laboured for your enrichment seven years, and I will not do so any longer if I can help it. I want to be free of you, and when you cancel the debt, my dearest hope will be never to see you again. Gouger."

Geoffrey scribbled his name. "Just get on, will you? I'm tired of your prattle." He watched Theo sign his own name, and handed him the contract. "Well then, let me hear it."

Theo slept, or dozed, on the settle in the taproom, huddled into himself against the chill night air, his face throbbing agonisingly. It meant he was roused by the first movements of the house, as yawning maids stumbled down to light the fires, but that was all to the good. He had work to do, and it had to be done as soon as possible.

He'd given his cousin a fine scare the previous night, spinning a tale of Martin's intended vengeance entirely from his fertile imagination. The only difficulty had been keeping himself from the wilder Gothic excesses that had presented themselves. Geoffrey had been quite ready to believe that Martin, with his faster carriage and greater resources, intended to overtake them, waylay them in some little-frequented stretch of road, and there mete out violent punishment for Geoffrey's sins.

Frankly, Martin probably could if he wished. Theo felt his stomach roil at the memory of those blows last night. The jarring impact, the pain of course, but mostly the set, terrible look on Martin's face as he'd struck. And the noise of it. Theo hadn't quite remembered how loud and sickening and *meaty* punches sounded.

He explored his swelling face with tentative fingers, cursed the bastard who'd decided to inflict this on him, and went off to bribe a stable hand in the matter of sabotaging Martin's chaise so that he could not pursue the larger, slower coach. He'd promised that to Geoffrey as part of their midnight scheming: he would ensure that Martin could not follow for hours, by chaise or hire of a horse. That would not be hard to achieve, he'd explained, here where Martin's colour would probably make him an object of suspicion anyway. A generous lubrication with what remained of the Conroys' money in Theo's pocket should ensure that the stable hands of the Farmers Arms would be slow and obstructive, and give the coach the best part of a day's head start. Martin would never catch up with them.

Them, because Theo was to come with Miss Conroy and Geoffrey. He'd insisted on that. "Do you think I wish to be left here alone with that brute?" he'd demanded. "He'll murder me!"

Geoffrey had made his lack of concern quite clear, but had acknowledged that Theo could make himself useful in other ways: making arrangements, bribing people on their route for silence, and otherwise allowing Geoffrey plenty of time to concentrate on keeping his intended bride up to the mark.

"She's shuffling," Geoffrey had said sourly. "Changing her mind, just like a woman. Wants her father at the wedding, wants a fine dress, wants this, wants that. It's a deal too late now, and so I let her know."

"As long as she says yes at the right moment," Theo had observed. "Otherwise we're all wasting our time here."

So Geoffrey was to spend the morning pressing kisses to Miss Conroy's fingertips and assuring her of his sentiments, and Theo was to be attendant, factotum, and—why not say it—henchman.

He spent a good half hour explaining to the stable hands what he wanted of them, receiving first disbelief, then roars of laughter as the unsubtle jest dawned upon them. By that time, Geoffrey and Miss Conroy had been roused and emerged into the inn yard, pallid and blinking in the morning sun. Neither appeared as though they had slept much better than Theo, and Miss Conroy's puffy eyes suggested that she had been crying.

They hurried through proceedings for departure. Theo glanced around nervously and repeatedly for interference, and saw from his cousin's twitches that his worry quickly became contagious. As Geoffrey handed, or bundled, Miss Conroy into their coach, Martin emerged from the inn, looking as though he'd thrown his clothes on. "You will wait here," he ordered Geoffrey savagely. "Don't you dare set off, sir. Ho, there, my horses!" He marched to the stables, bristling with impotent fury.

"They had better have done their work," Geoffrey said in Theo's ear.

Theo nudged him and indicated the ostler who stood, grinning, by them. "Is it as I asked?"

"Quite as you asked, sir. Oop, there he go."

As he spoke, Martin's full-throated bellow of fury echoed off the inn-yard walls. "What the devil do you *mean*, broken wheel shaft?"

The ostler gave a satisfied nod. "You be off now, sir. I dessay there'll be no traffic following you for a goodly while." He winked with great significance. Geoffrey handed him a shilling and made a noise of grudging approval in Theo's direction. It might have been as close as his cousin had ever come to thanking him.

The coach bowled off. Theo took the rumble seat, outside on the back, since Geoffrey had made it quite clear that he was not welcome inside. It was no hardship yet, except for the jolting: the air was fresh so early in the morning, the sun was bright but not yet too hot, there were birds chirruping and a pleasant breeze and a view over green fields and all that sort of bloody pastoral nonsense that people used to justify their misfortune in living outside London. It reminded Theo of the place that had once been his home, and he shut his eyes against that memory and turned his mind to the next book he had to write. A widow, with child, he'd decided, advertising for a husband and finding herself caught up in an inheritance scheme . . .

They stopped at a staging post, the White Hart, a little way outside Darlington. Theo let himself down from the rumble seat, stiff in every joint. Miss Conroy, stepping out of the coach, recoiled at the sight of his battered face. "Did Martin really hit you?" she demanded. "Why?"

"He didn't trust my intentions to you, miss. Which are none but the best, of course," Theo added with a servile bow. She gave him a look of frank distaste and swept away.

Naturally he was not welcome to take tea with the lovebirds in the parlour. He sat alone in the taproom, reading at a table that gave him a view of the corridor, and when Geoffrey went to the privy, he tucked the book into his pocket, and went to knock on the parlour door.

Miss Conroy sat alone, fingers knotted together. She did not seem pleased to see him enter. "What do you want?"

"I wished to see if I could apologise, Miss Conroy." Theo adopted his most obsequious stance. "I've clearly offended you with my presence and actions. But after all, we shall be cousins very soon, on the happy event of your nuptials."

Miss Conroy's expressive face made it clear this was a disadvantage of matrimony that had not previously occurred to her. Theo went on: "And as soon-to-be family, I hope we can cry friends. I assure you, I'm quite determined to see you married to Geoffrey." He smiled as widely as he could, knowing his mouth was distorted by the split lip. Miss Conroy flinched.

Theo gave her a chance to say something, some polite assurance or acknowledgement. She didn't, so he put a tiny bit of edge in his voice. "Miss, I hope you'll find it in your heart to look on me with more kindness, for Cousin Geoffrey's sake. Since we are now travelling companions and must perforce be friends." Her eyes widened a fraction, uncertain and distinctly uncomfortable. Theo smiled again. "Now, please accept a little token from me, eh? Something to pass the journey." He pulled the book from his pocket, ignoring the paper that fluttered out with it and onto the floor. "A romance, by Dorothea Swann. All about a couple flying to the border to marry. Just the thing, eh?" He handed her the book with a too-deep bow, smiled at her discomfited murmur of thanks, and left the room.

Geoffrey was in the corridor as Theo emerged, obviously impatient as the garrulous landlord talked at him. He scowled at Theo over the man's shoulder, and came up to him once he'd managed to remove himself from the one-sided conversation. "What were you doing in there?"

"I finished my book, so I thought I'd give it to Miss Conroy. Make her journey a little less tedious."

"I don't want you hanging around her. Keep yourself—"

There was a crash from inside the parlour, as of pottery broken with great force, and a shrill, rising shriek of fury. Geoffrey's eyes widened. "What the devil? Jennifer? Jennifer!"

He pulled the door open. Theo stepped back, heard Miss Conroy's enraged screech of "You horrible vile *pig*!" and retreated into the inn yard to find a stableboy.

Martin's chaise turned into the inn yard about five minutes after. By that time, Miss Conroy had backed Geoffrey outside and was still demolishing his character fluently and at impressive volume. Theo, along with half a dozen other people, watched with interest. His cousin, with a red handprint clear on his cheek, was still making a manful attempt to get a word in, but Theo wouldn't have wagered a shilling on his chances. Geoffrey had tried to steer his presumably erstwhile fiancée back inside to the private room and received another slap for his pains; the watching crowd had also stirred in a way that suggested they all took the young lady's side.

"Paying your horrible little cousin to get me to the altar!" Miss Conroy raged, disregarding the new arrival and waving the document under Geoffrey's nose like a sabre. "Bargaining with him! Bargaining! *Haggling*! Over *me*! You disgusting lying dirty cheating greedy miserly mean-spirited nasty *skinflint*!"

"Miss Conroy?" Martin's deep voice cut through the noise as he swung down from the chaise.

"Martin?" Miss Conroy's eyes widened, then she pushed Geoffrey aside, snatched up her skirts and hurled herself into Martin's arms as enthusiastically as any hero could have wished, burying her face in his shoulder. "Oh, Martin, Martin, thank heavens. Take me home. Please take me home."

"Of course I will." Martin gave her a gentle hug. "Are you well?"

"No!" She stepped back, face flushed, and indicated Geoffrey with a dramatic gesture. "He lied to me. He paid his horrible cousin to help him make me marry him, and he *bargained* about it!" Her voice cracked with distress, betraying a wounded heart that was, in Theo's estimation, very well seasoned with injured pride.

"Did you now," Martin said levelly, running his eyes over Geoffrey's person.

Geoffrey stepped back. "This is a misunderstanding. Don't you dare touch me. I will have the law on you."

"The lady is under age. You have been trying to force a marriage on her without her parents' consent and, it seems, by deception," Martin said. "I should very much like to have a magistrate hear what you have to say for yourself."

He advanced. Geoffrey took another step back, and found the watchers gathering in his way, preventing his escape. "This is a misrepresentation," he managed. "My sentiments—only the most sincere— If you touch me, I'll make her regret it! You know I can, and I will!"

Theo winced on his behalf. Miss Conroy's mouth opened in soundless horror. Martin stood, considering that, then he strode forward, grasped Geoffrey by the cravat, dragged him, struggling, sideways, and thrust his head down into the horse trough with a powerful hand. Geoffrey struggled violently, the water splashing around him. Martin pulled his head out, let him take a single breath, and dunked him again. This time he held him down until Geoffrey's struggles were spasmodic, then hauled him up, soaked and spluttering.

"You," Martin said, voice so low it seemed to vibrate in Theo's toes. "If you threaten the lady, so help me God . . ." He shook Geoffrey like a rat and dropped him onto the muck, dust, and straw of the inn yard, then turned on Theo. "And as for you, sir, you treacherous villain, you had best not cross my path again. At least there was one honest man among the bilkers you bribed to damage my vehicle, so your . . ." He hesitated a second, apparently in search of the mot juste. "Your plots were foiled. I leave the pair of you to one another and wish you joy of the company. Now get out of my sight."

He turned to Miss Conroy, evidently dismissing the cousins. Theo, for once, found himself the object of the crowd's disdainful gazes. It was not at all comfortable.

"You." Geoffrey pushed himself to hands and knees, staring at Theo with loathing. "You useless swine. When I get my hands on you . . ."

Theo looked at him, dripping, blotchy, shaking with rage and humiliation, and made a decision to walk back to the previous stage. It seemed unlikely he would be getting a free ride back south.

CHAPTER NINE

I t was seven endless days before Theo was back in the careless, filthy embrace of London. He let himself into his rooms on Little Wild Street, dropped his bag on the floor, and collapsed onto the chair, feeling his sense of relief tempered with an odd unfamiliarity, as if this place were no longer home.

The last week had been unspeakable. He'd been passed on the long trudge back to a staging post first by Martin and Miss Conroy, bowling along in the chaise, then, sometime later, by Geoffrey. He had stopped in order to let Theo know precisely what he thought of him and his unforgivable, clownish foolishness in dropping that fatal document, his failure to somehow rescue the situation, his inability even to bribe a stableboy properly, his broken promises. They had shouted at each other for some time, Geoffrey's hair drying unflatteringly over his skull in the sun, until at last Geoffrey had promised him that the bailiffs would be waiting when he returned to London, and drove off, leaving Theo alone once more, some three hundred miles from home, and with just a handful of coins in his pocket.

He'd paid for the stage, slept on floors, trudged miles on foot to husband the little money he had, and now, at last he was home. No bailiffs were to be seen yet, which was something, but they would doubtless come.

"Perhaps Geoffrey's been busy," he said to the cat that dozed on his windowsill as if it hadn't moved in his absence, and poured himself a drink. What with one thing and another, he thought he deserved it.

A week previously . . .

"I know I've given you no reason to treat my intentions with anything but contempt," Theo said, looking up into Martin's face. His breath came uncomfortably short; there seemed to be something constricting his chest. "But if I said I wanted to help, that I wanted to do better, would you trust me? Could you do that?"

"No," Martin said. "No, Theo, I don't think I could."

Theo sagged. Martin's fingers tightened on his scalp. "And yet, I have a terrible feeling that I'm going to anyway."

Theo's head came up so sharply that his hair pulled against Martin's grip. "Really?"

"Just tell me this. What is it that you want here?"

Theo thought about the bonds of debt and guilt under which he laboured, and how much of that weight he had made for himself. "I don't know. I have danced to the Hazelwood tune long enough, and I shall not do that any more. What I want . . . Oh, Martin, I am so tired of my life." He noted the widening of Martin's eyes and smiled weakly. "Not like that. I am tired of scrabbling and gouging and weaselling my way through life to scrape together pennies for Geoffrey's benefit. I am tired of the man I have become, and for such a foolish, sordid reason. A boy's stupidity, for which my life has grown warped. I prefer the man you thought I might be to the one I am. And, also, I realised that if Geoffrey is to do his worst anyway, if the sword suspended over my head is going to drop, there is no reason I should not do as I see fit now."

Martin nodded slowly. There was tension in his face. Not hostility—more as though he was hoping and trying not to hope. "And what seems fit?"

"Well," Theo said carefully. "I tried to think of what would happen if you were the hero in one of my novels, and the truth is, something would happen to help you along. Some chance, some ally. As you said, I'm not very good at writing heroes." He put his hand up to meet Martin's on his shoulder, felt Martin's fingers shift and flex a little. "So I wondered how you would feel about being the villain."

Martin took a few seconds to grasp his meaning, and then that glorious smile dawned, sending tingles across Theo's skin. "Because you are *excellent* at villains."

"I do have some small gift for scheming," Theo said modestly. "It just now occurred to me, you see, instead of thinking of how to rescue the maiden, I should be planning how to estrange the lovers, as a villain would. And . . . I have had an idea." He dared to interlace his fingers with Martin's a little more, and his heart skipped as they tightened in return. "I know it's not much, after everything, but may I plot for you, Martin?"

Martin pulled their hands off Theo's shoulder, fingers still entwined, and stooped to brush a kiss over Theo's knuckles. "My dear Mrs. Swann, my *very* dear Dorothea. Please do."

Coming up with a tale had been absurdly easy, once Theo had his way to tell the story. The only question had been whether he could make Geoffrey trust him, or at least believe he had changed sides again. Theo had been sure that he would seem quite convincing as long as he was sufficiently selfish and venal, and so it had proved. If he had begged for forgiveness or tried to offer repentance, Geoffrey would have seen through it at once. Greed, scorn, and insult were much easier to believe in than decency.

And, of course, proof of Theo's story was written in his face with its painful bruises.

That had been the hardest part of the whole affair. It had been damn near impossible to make Martin hit him, to the point where Theo had started wondering if he could assault himself, possibly by running into a bedpost. Martin had never hit anyone since boyhood, it turned out. He simply wasn't a violent man, and he'd ended up having to punch Theo four times, because he pulled the first two so much that they hadn't caused the needful damage. The blows had still hurt, as Theo had pointed out bitterly, and the next two had been damn near unbearable, leaving Theo rocking and whimpering on the floor, and Martin holding him, barely less distressed.

Martin holding him. He'd dropped to his knees without hesitation and put his arms around Theo, whispering appalled remorse, which Theo frankly felt he'd earned. He'd feared Martin might have broken his eye socket once the man had really thrown his weight behind the blow.

But it had needed doing. Geoffrey was no brawler, and the sight of Theo's battered features had been enough to unnerve him on its own. Then there had been the late hour and his sleep-addled mind; the high stakes he played for; Theo's defiance and aggression, turning the established order of things on its head. Theo had unsettled him in all the ways he could, and once the ground was broken, he'd seeded it with threats of Martin's intended vengeance. He'd gone to town there, playing on Geoffrey's fears of retribution with dark threats of Martin's uncivilised, vengeful nature. After all, it was common knowledge that men of colour were violent and dangerous, and Geoffrey's mind was as common as they came.

That had been the easiest part: using Geoffrey's nature against him. Theo knew how much his cousin hated to give up what he had, how ready he was to suspect others of sharp practice because it was exactly what he would do himself. It had obviously not occurred to him that Theo would sacrifice his own freedom and profit for Miss Conroy's sake.

And he'd been right, because of course that wasn't why Theo had done it.

The rest had been simple, if nerve-wrenching. He had bribed the stable hand at the Farmers Arms to seem to be about his business while not actually damaging Martin's chaise, and the postilion to stop at a list of stages gleaned from the landlady and passed to Martin. He'd also had a stableboy at the White Hart sent out when they stopped, ready to flag Martin's chaise down, just in case. Then he had merely needed to find a way to drop the incriminating contract convincingly, and watch the sparks fly right into the powder magazine.

Martin had insisted that he should not simply give Miss Conroy the contract and that they should keep up the pretence of enmity to the end. There was, he'd pointed out, nothing to be gained from making Geoffrey see how he'd been fooled, and it might potentially be of some use if he believed Theo was still on his side. Geoffrey hadn't, but at least it seemed he had not yet put court proceedings for debt in motion.

That would come, Theo knew. His chances of persuading his cousin to mercy were small to the point of nonexistent, and he was quite sure the Conroys would not prosecute Geoffrey for abduction or rape if it could be avoided, which was to say, if Miss Conroy was not with child. They would not wish to advertise her lost maidenhead, after all. No, Geoffrey would have plenty of opportunity to revenge himself on Theo, and there was no doubt in Theo's mind that he would.

He went to get a pitcher of water for a much-needed wash, dug out some reasonably clean clothes, and then sat down to look around the little, crowded office where he'd slept and worked for four years. It had felt like a prison often enough, but now that the shadows of a real prison loomed over him, he discovered the place was really very tolerable.

Tolerable, but empty. It had looked better with Martin in it.

He wasn't here now, but perhaps he might have written. Theo heaved his tired bones out of the chair at that thought and hurried downstairs to pick up his letters from the Three Ducks. The mass of paper required a sack, and he tipped the lot out onto the floor of his office and sorted through it at speed, looking only at the addresses.

Everything was to the *Matrimonial Advertiser*. There was no personal letter for Theo Swann; nothing but a great slew of pleas and promises from the lonely and the desperate, the deceptive and the painfully sincere, the people making a mockery of love and the ones who never gave up hope of it. Nothing but advertisements. Nothing from Martin.

Theo had thought he might have written, that was all. Just to let him know how things had proceeded, to say if their scheme had worked, if Mr. Conroy had been grateful. Martin must have been back in London for days, since the stage had plodded along at barely more than walking speed. He would have had time to write, if he'd wanted.

Theo sat at his desk, looking at the wall opposite and making himself understand that Martin had not wanted to write. Then he began opening the advertisements, because even if he was to sit here alone and waiting to be arrested for debt, business was business.

A gentleman of mature years sought a young lady. A farmer wished for a wife. A publican's widow wanted a husband experienced in the running of an inn. A lady marred by smallpox, a gentleman with more fashion than funds, the usual parade of characters passed over his desk, hour after hour. The cat on his windowsill slept and woke, yawned and stretched, investigated the papers and grew bored and wandered away, leaving Theo alone in a pile of dreams.

The clock had struck five when he unfolded the next advertisement.

WANTED, A Gentleman of better character than he knows, who plays the Villain to the manner born. Prompt application to M.St.V. is greatly desired as a Promise remains to be kept.

Theo read that three times, in a calm, sensible, rational way, making quite sure he understood its meaning, and then ran down the stairs so fast he almost tripped over the cat.

Martin had penned the advertisement several days ago, smiling as he did it, imagining Theo's amusement. His own had faded day by day as he'd waited for any sort of response. First he'd told himself that the stage would take at least twice the time of the travelling chaise he'd used to whisk Miss Jennifer back to her parents. Then he'd started to fret over imaginings—if Theo had been left with enough funds to travel back to London, if his cousin had attacked him, or found some way to use the law against him up north where Theo had nobody to call on. Finally, this morning it had dawned on him that the *Matrimonial Advertiser*'s postbag must by now be so large that his own jest might easily be buried under a mound of sincere communications. He was composing a letter to be delivered directly when the knock came, and his housekeeper poked her head around the door.

"There's a Mr. Swann to see you."

Martin carefully wiped the nib and replaced the pen on the desk. "Show him into the parlour please, Peggy, and—I think you may go for the day after that."

Peggy's brows rose. "Can I, now?"

"Yes. Go on."

"Well, I shan't say no, if you'd like to be left alone." Peggy pursed her lips. "Hmm. I wonder."

"What?"

"If you're going to stop looking like a hungry dog every time there's a knock at the door that turns out to be the butcher. Is this a game one, then?"

Martin gave her the most threatening look he could manage. It had no effect whatsoever. Peggy had been with him for twelve years, growing from a scrawny, scrappy brat to a well-built woman of decided personality. She had somehow absorbed the knowledge of his desires along the way, and had moved from silent support to enthusiastic encouragement of any romance she could see or imagine. There had been nothing of that nature in his life for a full three years, and he had a lowering feeling that if things did not go well now, she would demand an explanation tomorrow.

She was smirking at him, obviously convinced of her own deductions. He sighed. "Be off with you, wench."

Peggy shot him a saucy wink, murmured, "Enjoy yourself," and danced down the hall, doubtless planning to spend her free evening with her own sweetheart. Martin put a couple of things in his pockets, squared his shoulders, and went in to the parlour, and Theo.

He was there, out of breath and dishevelled as he'd been the first time he'd come running to Martin's door. Sitting on the edge of a chair, looking up at Martin with those rainy-sky eyes, one still puffy with the green spread of bruise, and a tension in his sinewy body that set Martin's own nerves twanging.

"Good afternoon," he managed, shutting the door behind him. Theo rose awkwardly, evidently unsure what to say. Martin felt as hesitant. "I'm pleased to see you. I wasn't sure if you were going to come."

"I only reached home at noon," Theo said. "And I only saw your advertisement just now."

Martin winced. "I'm sorry. It seemed like an amusing thing to do, until I realised how many you must receive."

"It was buried quite deep. So." He stuck his hands in his pockets and rocked on his toes. "How is Miss Conroy?"

"She's well. Rather chastened, I think, by her adventure. Very glad to be home, and her parents are glad to have her there."

"And will there be, uh, consequences to her escapade?"

"It seems not." Martin had had a long and excessively frank talk with Miss Jennifer on the way back, touching on the subjects of men, menses, and motherhood, since she seemed to have been kept in a state of profound ignorance about all three. He'd decided she should at least know what the future was likely to bring and, thanks be, it had brought her monthlies just a day later. It was the second time Martin had had to explain the facts of life to a young lady, his first being with Peggy, and he lived in hope that he would never have to do it again. "As long as Hazelwood keeps his silence, all should be well."

"And will he?" Theo asked. "Has Mr. Conroy paid him off? He's a fairly desperate man."

"Yes, well, that was difficult." Martin made a face. They'd had to tell Miss Jennifer's father of her disgrace, since it was all too likely that Hazelwood would use it. He had responded as one might have expected, with anger, shame, and blame, raging his refusal to pay the damned blackmailing swine a penny, until Martin had made a suggestion. "Mr. Conroy did not wish to reward his villainy directly. So he's bought Felford Hall."

Theo's eyes widened. "He what?"

"Bought the family home, for a sum that leaves Hazelwood unencumbered and with a decent amount to live on. Many would say your cousin has done very well for himself."

"He's sold the Hall," Theo said slowly. "Did he—did he *want* to?"

"Not at all, no. He raged and even wept, but Mr. Conroy was not to be moved. It was that or nothing, he said. I have you to thank for that idea, as for so much else," he added. "Mr. Conroy was quite reconciled to paying him off as long as it hurt."

"It will have done," Theo said. "Believe me."

Martin felt not a grain of remorse. Miss Jennifer had wept on his shoulder until the cloth was soaked. He'd have supported Mr. Conroy in having Hazelwood beaten to jelly.

"Well, he made the bargain. We had a few other concessions out of him for the money, also. A written statement that we can use against him if he impugns Miss Jennifer's reputation. And, er, this."

He withdrew the folded paper from his pocket and held it out. Theo took it, opened it, and read.

Martin had indulged in fantasies of him reading it for several days, of how he would react when he saw Hazelwood's affidavit that the debt was cancelled. Theo's reaction was nothing like the dramatic joy he had pictured. He stood still, a little frown creasing his forehead, and then he raised his eyes to meet Martin's gaze, and Martin's chest constricted as though embraced by a bear.

"Did . . ." Theo licked his lips. "Did you do this?"

"Mr. Conroy did. I told Miss Jennifer the truth of your actions—we had a long journey, a long time to talk. She has matured a little over the last days, I suspect. She was adamant that the family owed you a great deal." And had clearly realised that it would enrage Geoffrey Hazelwood to lose his hold over his cousin. Martin couldn't fault her motivation. "She spoke well for you. I merely added my voice."

Theo was shaking his head. "I didn't do anything for her sake or her family's. Martin, tell me you did not have to ask this as a favour. Tell me you don't owe them this. *Please.* I will tear this agreement up if that's what it means. I would rather do that, for my own soul's sake if nothing else. I will not be responsible for that."

Martin closed his eyes. He couldn't answer for a second, not with those words in his ears. Theo with relief of the debt in his grasp, and ready to give it up for him.

"*Martin,*" Theo said.

"No. You need not worry about accepting it."

He couldn't deny that Mr. Conroy had looked to him, waited for him to speak, before he agreed to Miss Jennifer's request. He had wanted to grant Martin a favour, find a way to balance the books, and he had paid Theo's debt as a means of paying Martin, whether he wanted payment or not. That was very clear, and the extraordinary thing was, it had barely mattered at all. "I added my voice to Miss Jennifer's, and that is all. I didn't have to; I chose to. I daresay Mr. Conroy thought of it as a way of restoring the order of things." Theo's face twisted. Martin took his hand, rubbing his thumb over the palm, feeling his thin fingers curl. "But, Theo, I don't care."

"Truly?" Theo sounded stifled, disbelieving.

"Let Mr. Conroy believe he purchased his daughter's safety if it makes him feel better. If he cannot accept a friend's help without making it a transaction, I am sorry for it, but that is his affair. I acted as I thought best, and I owe the Conroys nothing. Not for this, not for anything." It wasn't as simple as the saying of it, but it was true, and for the first time he felt that one day he would believe that. He looked into Theo's troubled eyes. "And you owe me nothing either, in case you're wondering."

"Seven hundred pounds," Theo said, choked.

"You earned it. You risked your liberty and your future for Miss Conroy."

"I did nothing for her sake."

"You helped me, we helped her, Mr. Conroy helped you. That is how it should be."

"I'm fairly sure he didn't want to help me to the tune of seven hundred pounds."

"But I wanted him to, and he owes me that." Martin heard the note of steel in his own voice, saw Theo's eyes widen at it. He deliberately made his tone lighter. "And in any case . . ." He brought his other hand to Theo's face, with its fading bruises. "Dorothea Swann lives by her work, does she not? Consider your story a private commission, paid accordingly. A drama written for four."

Theo's cheek muscles moved under his palm as, at last, a smile dawned. "I should write for private audiences more often, at this rate of pay. What is it: *Jennifer: or, Villainy Triumphant?*"

"*Theodore: or, Virtue Finally Located.*"

Theo tucked the paper into his inside pocket. His now-free hand slid downward, over Martin's belly, brushing the front of his breeches. "*Finally Located, and Promptly Discarded.*"

"An excellent choice," Martin said, a little hoarsely. Theo's hand was between his legs, cupping him, and he let his fingers spread wide over the narrow face he held. "Theo . . ."

"I have to raise something." Theo's voice wobbled slightly.

"What?"

"'Your plots were foiled'? Did you really say that out loud?"

Martin began to laugh. "Dear heaven, don't remind me. I couldn't think of what to say, and we were acting a melodrama anyway."

"Just promise me that you'll leave the literary composition to me in future."

"You have my word." Martin leaned a little closer. "Talking of promises . . ."

"We have unfinished business?"

Martin gently tilted Theo's chin up. "A great deal of it. I don't want to finish our business today, or at any time soon. You talked about the man you wanted to be and the one I thought you to be, but in truth, I like the man you are. The one in front of me now. I want to know you when we're not both being jolted to pieces or chasing around the countryside. And I very much want to see you on your hands and knees, naturally, but that's not all I want, and I hope it's not all you want."

Theo's lips were slightly parted, the bottom one still a little discoloured at the corner from Martin's blow. "No," he said, on a breath. "That's not all I want either. I didn't know if I could have more."

"You have a new start." Martin ran his fingers through Theo's fine hair, loving the feel of it, as Theo's hand slid up to his hip, not so much seductive as simply holding on. "I wonder if we might start together, perhaps. Find out how we get on."

"See what happens?"

"Learn a little more of each other."

Theo nodded. "Right. Yes. You are going to fuck me, aren't you?"

"Definitely."

"Just making sure." Theo leaned against him. Martin disengaged his hand to put his arms round the slim shoulders with a peculiar feeling of relief; Theo's hands went round his own waist in return. "I'm not quite sure of what I'm doing otherwise."

Martin kissed his hair. "Well, it's a good place to start."

Theo lifted his face, and their mouths met. Martin kissed him carefully, soft movements, just reacquainting himself with Theo's taste and feel. Theo's mouth was once again a little tentative, as if he wasn't quite sure of the steps of this dance, but his hands on Martin's waist were decided in their clasp, and after a few moments, they moved from decided to determined. Theo's fingers spread, digging in, his mouth widened, and Martin followed the lead, kissing him harder now, wanting to feel him bend and give.

Theo bit at his lip, dragging his teeth over the soft flesh. Martin grabbed for the hands clamped on his arse and moved them to hold Theo's arms together behind his back, Martin's hands over his. Theo tilted his hips provocatively forward, and Martin pulled him tighter until the sensation of thighs and bellies and pricks colliding was nigh unbearable and he had an urgent need to rid them both of the layers of clothing in their way. Theo was grinding against him, making his wants vividly clear, mouth greedy and sloppy and warm, and Martin had a sudden terror he might spend before he was even unclothed.

He grunted into Theo's mouth, tugged on his hands. Theo bent away at the hips, keeping their lower bodies pressed. "Mmm?"

"I want you naked," Martin said, voice startling even him with its low growl.

"In here?" Theo glanced at the window.

The parlour was at the back of the house, and the yard his alone, but still, better safe than sorry. Martin gave him a gentle push, releasing his hands. "If you close the shutters?"

Theo scampered to do that, while Martin lit a lamp. They turned back to each other in the dimmer light. Theo looked absurdly, gloriously wanton, with his dishevelled hair and his prick straining for release.

"Undress," Martin said. "I want to watch you."

Theo's mouth curved. He shed his coat with a quick motion, tossing it onto a chair, and pulled the loose shirt over his head, linen billowing to cover his face, belly bared to Martin's view. He jerked his shoestrings undone, kicked away the shoes, and stripped off his stockings with little more ceremony.

"Stop." Martin walked up to him and spanned his belly with both hands, thumbs touching. He slid them up and down, over Theo's thin chest with its sparse hair; over the small, pale nipples; over the wings of his rib cage and the dent of his navel and the jut of his hip bones. Just touching, learning, feeling Theo's hungry eyes on his face.

"Perfect," he murmured.

Theo gave a breathy laugh. "That is very far from the truth."

"Perfect for me."

Theo's expression shifted slightly to something a little puzzled, a little wondering. "Well . . . If you say so?"

"It is past time you learn that I mean what I say." Martin bent forward and sucked deliberately at his neck, with lips and teeth together. Theo whimpered. "Now strip."

Theo squirmed out of his trousers and drawers together so that he stood bare and hard and waiting. Martin wanted to whimper himself. Instead he went to his knees, taking hold of Theo's hips with both hands, and put his mouth to Theo's stand. Just lightly, but the hips he held jerked as though he'd taken him down in a gulp, and Theo's hands slid and scrabbled for a grip on his own cropped hair. Martin took his time, licking and kissing and mouthing around Theo's prick without ever engulfing it, and by the time his own constricted prick could bear no more, Theo was moaning abjectly.

Martin pushed himself to his feet and stripped, fingers feeling swollen and clumsy, and considerably hindered by Theo's assistance in tugging at his shirt and fumbling at his buttons. Between them they got the clothing off at last. Martin kicked away his drawers, and Theo pressed himself close, joining their nakedness.

"Martin," he said. "This has been a delightful interlude, but if you don't fuck me right now, I am going to set fire to your house. Consider yourself warned."

"Well, if you put it that way." Martin got his hands across Theo's arse and walked him backward, to the settle. "How do you like it?"

Theo wrapped one leg around Martin's thigh. "In."

"I'm trying to treat you with respect and consideration," Martin pointed out. "The least you could do is stop playing the harlot."

"What makes you think I'm playing?"

"Tomcat."

They grinned at each other. Theo's eyes were at once dark with lust and bright with pleasure, and Martin's heart stuttered at the open happiness he saw.

"Over the settle?" he suggested. Theo shifted round obligingly, and Martin retrieved a bottle of oil from the desk, where he'd put it several very long days ago, and knelt behind him. He stroked Theo's thighs, back, between his legs, feeling him twist and push back. Slicked a finger to probe deeper and open him up a little.

"I know what I'm doing," Theo said, a little breathlessly.

"Probably better than I," Martin admitted.

Theo glanced round. "Oil yourself. Oh, Jesus, that looks so good. Just keep doing that." His eyes were fixed on Martin's hand as he stroked himself, his stand glistening with oil. "I could watch you do that all day."

"I'll make a memorandum," Martin rasped, letting his palm slide under his length for the pure pleasure of Theo's look.

Theo shifted his legs wider. "Ready? Come forward, and on my word." His head tipped back. "Now."

Martin pushed into him, with no more than a little difficulty. Theo was tight and warm, and he groaned and arched his back in a way that went straight to Martin's bollocks.

"God, God, *God*, yes. Again, deeper. Slow. *There.*"

Martin gripped his shoulders, breathing deeply. Theo squirmed back against him, as best he could, and Martin splayed a hand over his back in a futile effort to keep him still. He grasped Theo's hip with his other hand, and took a moment longer to regain control, and to learn the thin, sharp lines of Theo's back, and admire the way his skin looked against Theo's in the light of the oil lamp. Like marquetry: gleaming mahogany inlaid in the lightest birchwood, or perhaps the other way around. Laid together.

"You look so good like this," he whispered.

"On my knees with your prick in my arse?"

"Born for it."

Martin began to move, slowly at first, finding his pace. Theo moved as well, more than any of the few partners Martin had had previously, picking up the rhythm. His back flexed, his shoulders worked. Martin leaned into him, pressing his lips to Theo's neck, felt him arch.

"Harder." The sound vibrated through his neck and Martin's lips. He kissed, bit, thrust as he did it, and Theo's hair whipped as he jerked his head back, and then the pair of them were moving at once in a controlled frenzy of desire and sensation, push and pull, bodies heaving together, slicked with sweat. Martin got his hand round to Theo's prick, and Theo drove into his fist, snarling and gasping as he fucked Martin's hand and was fucked in turn, and when Martin spent inside him, it was with a cry of almost-pain for the blinding sharpness of the sensation that shot through him.

His hand was wet with Theo's spend, he realised, so he allowed himself to collapse forward, face resting on Theo's sweaty back.

"And you say that was merely the start," Theo said at last. "I'll be dead by next Tuesday."

Martin tugged him closer, kissing his ear. "But what a magnificent end."

"Yours is rather appealing too," Theo assured him. Martin gave him a swat, and they ended up lolling together on the settle, hot, sticky, bone-tired, limbs entangled, and mouths close enough to kiss or talk.

"Tell me," Theo said after an interlude of the former. "Was that a phantasm born of panic, or is my debt truly cancelled?"

"In full."

"That . . ." There was a little puzzled frown between Theo's brows. "I'm rather struggling to understand that. It's been there for so long. I thought it would always be there. And it's gone, and now I'm not quite sure what to do."

Martin dropped a kiss on his hair. "Well, it seems to me your best course is simply to pursue your occupation. Not that I have any ulterior motive in the suggestion, of course, but I have been looking forward to Mrs. Swann's next work, so if you did happen to be thinking of a new book . . ."

"I have one just gone to the publisher actually, and an idea I've been toying with." Theo paused. "And I can take a little time to write it. Not feel Geoffrey breathing down my neck. Do better work. I might even write a half-decent hero. My *God.*"

"You've the world before you. It's quite a big place, once you can raise your head and see it."

"Mmm." Theo's eyes were wide and happy, the colour of one of those cold, drizzly days that preceded a glorious spring, and Martin didn't think he could recall a shade he liked more. "Will you show me around?"

Martin smiled down at him. "Let's look together."

AUTHOR'S NOTE

This story was inspired by a display in the excellent "Black Georgians: The Shock of the Familiar" exhibition run by the Black Cultural Archives in London. It told the story of Cesar Picton (1755?–1836), an emancipated black Briton who remained on sociable terms with the family of his former enslaver, and asked how apparently friendly relationships of this kind might have felt to those involved.

Any errors are, of course, of my own making.

Dear Reader,

Thank you for reading KJ Charles's *Wanted, A Gentleman*!

We know your time is precious and you have many, many entertainment options, so it means a lot that you've chosen to spend your time reading. We really hope you enjoyed it.

We'd be honored if you'd consider posting a review—good or bad—on sites like **Amazon, Barnes & Noble, Kobo, Goodreads, Twitter, Facebook, Tumblr,** and your blog or website. We'd also be honored if you told your friends and family about this book. Word of mouth is a book's lifeblood!

For more information on upcoming releases, author interviews, blog tours, contests, giveaways, and more, please sign up for our weekly, spam-free newsletter and visit us around the web:

Newsletter: tinyurl.com/RiptideSignup
Twitter: twitter.com/RiptideBooks
Facebook: facebook.com/RiptidePublishing
Goodreads: tinyurl.com/RiptideOnGoodreads
Tumblr: riptidepublishing.tumblr.com

Thank you so much for Reading the Rainbow!

RiptidePublishing.com

ACKNOWLEDGEMENTS

With thanks to Julio-Alexi Genao and C. Morgan Kennedy, to Anne Scott, and to the fine people at Riptide.

The history of lonely hearts advertising is treated in detail in the wonderfully entertaining *Shapely Ankle Preferr'd* by Francesca Beauman.

ALSO BY
KJ CHARLES

A Charm of Magpies world
The Magpie Lord
A Case of Possession
Flight of Magpies
Jackdaw
A Queer Trade
Rag and Bone

Society of Gentlemen
The Ruin of Gabriel Ashleigh
A Fashionable Indulgence
A Seditious Affair
A Gentleman's Position

Non-Stop Till Tokyo
Think of England
The Secret Casebook of Simon Feximal

Sins of the Cities
An Unseen Attraction (Feb 2017)

ABOUT
THE AUTHOR

KJ Charles is a writer and freelance editor. She lives in London with her husband, two kids, an out-of-control garden, and an increasingly murderous cat.

KJ writes mostly romance, mostly queer, frequently historical, and usually with some fantasy or horror in there.

Find her on Twitter @kj_charles, pick up free reads on her website at kjcharleswriter.com, get the infrequent newsletter at kjcharleswriter.com/newsletter, or join her Facebook group, KJ Charles Chat, for sneak peeks and exclusives.

She is represented by Courtney Miller-Callihan at Handspun Literary.

Enjoy more stories like
Wanted, A Gentleman
at RiptidePublishing.com!

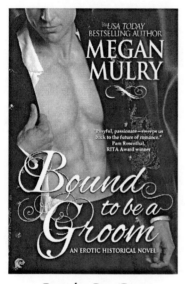

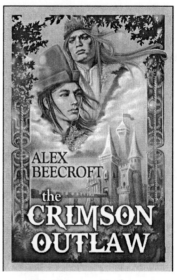

Bound to Be a Groom
ISBN: 978-1-62649-113-7

The Crimson Outlaw
ISBN: 978-1-62649-053-6

Earn Bonus Bucks!

Earn 1 Bonus Buck for each dollar you spend. Find out how at
RiptidePublishing.com/news/bonus-bucks.

Win Free Ebooks for a Year!

Pre-order coming soon titles directly through our site and you'll
receive one entry into a drawing for a chance to win free books for
a year! Get the details at RiptidePublishing.com/contests.

CPSIA information can be obtained
at www.ICGtesting.com
Printed in the USA
LVOW08s1819100317
526810LV00002B/484/P